5-Minute Short Stories of Love, Betrayal, Reflection, and Humor

by

J. Paulette Forshey

All characters in this book have no existence outside the imagination of the author and have no relation whatsoever to anyone bearing the same name or names. They are not even distantly inspired by any individual known or unknown to the author, and all incidents are pure invention. Published by: T-Bear Enterprises.

"Pirates will be hunted down and shot in the street like the dogs they are."

Print – ISBN: 979-8-9945997-0-9
E-Book – ISBN: 979-8-9945997-1-6

Publisher: T-Bear Enterprises
Cover Designer: Cindy Stonebrook
Paul Salvette –
Managing Director BB eBooks bbebooksthailand.com

Dedicated to

To friends: the late Pam Ritchie – editor, Cindy Stonebrook confident and excellent cover artist, Samantha Barker and Beverly Justice editors and beta readers, and the Cambridge Writers for all their support.

My loving husband, who always thought I had potential and was proud of me, love you, now and forever.

The poem Valentines 'Not One Day a Year' is for Dennis.

Table of Contents

NOSTALGIC

UNCLE EUGENE

YOU'LL HAVE TO ignore Uncle Eugene when he begins to stare and mumble. Since his 'experience'. That's what kin calls it, Uncle Eugene just hasn't been right in the head. Not saying he was before but well before we just thought he was a little slow. Uncle Eugene's problems got worse after the 'experience.

It started one dark and stormy night and Uncle Eugene and Fred, that's Uncle Eugene's Redbone Coon Hound, were alone in the cabin. According to Uncle Eugene, everything was fine. He had a cozy fire going, rabbit stew with fresh greens, and sweet baby onions in the pot. Uncle Eugene's partial to sweet baby onions. The roof and the wall chinking were tight and dry. Alice Kirby been by earlier and left them a criss-cross apple pie, you see before his 'experience' she was sweet on him.

Well, there was Uncle Eugene and Fred all cozy as a hog in deep mud. Uncle Eugene was just headed from the table with his plate to fill it when the lantern and the fire went out. That was just plum strange because Uncle Eugene yousta to make a good fire. A log made a snap and a pop in the hearth. That's when old Fred growled low and deep in his throat. You know that kinda sound when a Red Bone corners something a lot bigger than hisself. That's when everything else gets real quiet and the hair sticks up on the back of your neck and arms. It was that sound. Well, there stood Uncle Eugene, not sure to go forward or back and Fred keeps growling then starts moving around the room.

Uncle Eugene couldn't hear anything but the wind and rain and old Fred growling that growl. Then the cabin door busted open and something come tumbling in.

Well, let me tell you Uncle Eugene was pretty scared about then. Fred must have latched on to the thing, and it must have latched on to Fred. Uncle Eugene said there were all kind of growling, howling, and chomp'n. There Uncle Eugene stood not sure to go forward or back with all that going on around him. He said it was if the Devil himself had latched on to a Catamount's tail. The fighten continued for aways then old Fred and the thing went barreling out the busted cabin door. Then it got real quiet. Real scary quiet.

Uncle Eugene said he stood there listen to the wind, rain, and the quiet in the cabin. Then the lantern and the fire flared back up. The cabin was all teared up, the cook pot was licked clear clean and so was the pie tin.

Uncle Eugene just stood there looking at his tore up cabin 'til first light not sure if he should go forward or back. That's how we found him three days later. We brung him down to our place and offered him the spare bed, seeing his kin and all but come night fall Uncle Eugene went and barricade hisself in our shed. Every morning now, he comes out and sits on our front porch. He eats his meals there, rocking hisself in a chair that doesn't do that. Then come nightfall, off he goes to the shed. He don't trouble anyone most times. Uncle Eugene just been stuck like that in his head not sure if he should go forward or back. Until he decides I guess he'll be living in our shed. That's ok, his kin and all.

Well, if you'll excuse me I better it those squezzins to help Uncle Eugene with his 'experience'. 'Til then you'll have to ignore Uncle Eugene.

Deep Cut Murder

This is a fictional piece based on facts taken from the book *Stories of Guernsey County Ohio* by Wolfe, 1943, page eight-hundred-sixteen, paragraph seven of *Center Township.*

"I, THE REV. I. M. Goode, do vow on this third day of June, in the year of our Lord eighteen-hundred and fifty, that the following confession was given to me by one Joseph Bartholomew Milner. To be sent in his own words, to the Justice of the Peace of Cambridge, Ohio, in the hope that terrible wrong may finally be righted."

I, Joseph Bartholomew Milner, do wish to go to meet my maker with a clear conscience. I have committed many a crime in my misguided, miserable life, things like theiven' horses, breakin' in of people's homes, rollin' drunken old men and taken liberties with several fine upstandin' young ladies. But the one thing that has been weighin' heavy on me ever since me and Seth, me baby sister's man, done it, was the day we kilt a woman in Ohio. I swear as God is my witness we never meaned to kilt her, just rob her.

Me baby sister Mary and her man Seth, which I has mentioned before, lives a couple-a-miles east of a town named Cambridge, in Ohio, There be a tavern by the name of Deep Cut. So bein' named cause of its bein' cut deep in a hill few feet off'n the road National.

Me and Seth had been a-drinkin' at the tavern one night when a lady comes in askin' for a room. She was a-totin' a big old saddle bag. Seth thought she might be a-carryin' money or jewels. Me and Seth kept a-drinkin' and discussin' that there lady's bag most of the night.

The next mornin' early we waited down the road a piece in the woods 'tilin' she goes by. We could tell she was l real lady 'cause she was a-ridin' side saddle. This bein' we was surprised when she kicked up such a fight when we grabbed the horse's reins.

She was a hollarin' and swiggin' at us with her ridin' crop. She caught me once good on a-side of my head. I was tryin' to grab the dang thing when her horse step side-a-ways right in a gopher hole. The lady loses her seat and fell hard. Seth hurries over to her. She was a-layin' kinda funny and real quiet-like. Seth says she's dead, must a-hit her head real bad. So we gets scared and takes her body upin' the woods and buries her. Then we turns her horse loose after we takes off its leather.

Me and Seth feels even badder when we opens that there saddle bag. She was only totin' clothes and a few gold coins. Later, I's heard that folks at the tavern got blamed fer the lady's death.

Well, now, Seth's long been gone an I's about to meet my maker. I just wants to clear things befoein' I go.

Joseph Bartholomew Milner

Dutifully recorded by the Rev. I. M. Goode at the penitentiary of Alton, Illinois.

SIMPLER TIMES

I STOOD BEFORE the old building taking in every boarded-up window and doorway. In the stillness of the morn, one could hear a weary sigh escape from its aged walls.

Was it really that many years ago when children's voices and laughter filled its rooms and halls? Reciting math facts, learning 'I' before 'E' except after 'C' or pledging their allegiance to the flag.

Now large ugly red signs proclaiming, 'Warning This Building Unsafe', 'Condemned' scar is doors.

I remember the building, the laughter and smell. If I close my eyes, I can still inhale the scent of chalk and fresh washed blackboards. There were desks of real wood, inkwells intact, with big brother or sister's initials carved in the top.

Freshly waxed floors and woodwork gleamed in the sun. The kindly old custodian who kept it all clean, he whittled whistles of wood for those who found the right size twigs. I remember the teachers who taught not only older siblings but mother and dad too. They remembered how well dad *really* did in history and math.

We've replaced all this with plastic and steel. My children now have green boards, with soft pastels of colored chalk. All proven much better for the eyes. My children now learn a mouse helps with a computer and isn't just a small furry eater of cheese. Oh, remember Dick and Jane? They have careers now. They once played with trucks and dolls.

They're tearing it down next week for a mall. I had hoped my children would know it as I. Now my memories and stories must keep it alive. Oh, for simpler days, simpler times.

Pleasant Street

My name is Jane. Yes, I am *that,* Jane. I was once married to Dick, excuse me, Richard. Everyone thought we were the perfect couple. Well, *everyone* wasn't there late at night when the lights went off and the arguing started.

My name is Richard. When I was a child people called me Dick. I am told a name is a name and a rose by any other name is still a rose. Whoever said either didn't work in high tech (stress) business. My first wife still insists on calling me Dick. She had the looks that could have taken us both far, but she just didn't have what it takes to make it in my world. It isn't enough anymore to *just* be good at your job, you must live and breathe it, too. Sometimes even that isn't enough.

Dick wanted children. Well I hadn't spent

four years in college, working part time during each semester and summers in an advertising firm at the same time, just so I could get pregnant and stay home.

Yes, I married Jane and divorced her too. She wanted a career. That's fine, but she should have thought about helping me with mine. I needed a wife and two children. The married guys are the first to get promotions and the first to get invited to the boss's summer place in the Hamptons for a weekend. Jane just didn't understand how much I could have used her.

Dick never could understand I was just as serious about my career as he was about his.

All right, so I didn't have to work while I was in college. I did belong to the same fraternity as my father, Dad's money did help me, so what money talks, all you have to do is let it whisper in the right ears.

Well, I got the job I wanted. I worked hard for it. I paid my dues and believe me, a woman in this field pays her dues. I work for one of the most prestigious advertising agencies in New York City. I make enough money so that I can live in a condo in the right part of the city. I even had it decorated by the same designer that did my boss's condo. The entire condo is very chic, very correct.

I really enjoy the place when I am home… which isn't much.

Thanks to money and the right people I have what I want. It helped me marry, finally, the right woman. I married the company's vice-president's daughter. Heck, I would have married the boss's daughter if he had one.

I travel a lot, but I always stay in the right hotels. I usually have my assistant call one of the male escort services when she makes all my other reservations. I use the escort for a dinner companion. A woman goes through too much hassle if she tries to dine alone.

Ann's a great woman, nothing like Jane. Oh sure, some say after the nose job I insisted, Anne have, she looks something like Jane, well maybe, but that's all.

No, I never do anything else with my escort. That would be tacky. Besides, I usually go back to my room and work on the next day's presentation. I know plenty of male co-workers who do sleep around but I see how it affects their jobs. I've worked too hard to let something like that come between my career and me. If I want a good work out, I go to the gym.

Ann's a real whiz at seating just the right people next to each other at our dinner parties. Ann does her part for my career; she spends her days with her women's groups and lets me know who's doing what to whom. The last bit of information she gave me closed a particularly messy deal rather nicely. Ann produced two children right away and with our health club membership, she is a size smaller now than on her wedding day.

Sure, sometimes I think about having children, but if I were to take time off, I'd lose my position and status. I haven't even taken a week's vacation in five years.

My children are great. I am sending them to the finest private schools in the state. Ann sees to it that the au pair has the children fed and ready for bed an hour after I am home. That way we can discuss priorities for the next day uninterrupted.

Time is money and money is time. Men don't have to take time off to have children. They don't have to take time off when the child is sick or for parent/teacher conferences.

The bonus I received on the deal from Ann's information helped pay for the last decorator she hired. It also helped pay to have Jill's place redone too. Ann knows about Jill, but she doesn't make a fuss about it. I just hope Ann's father doesn't find out, that would finish my career.

Well, I've worked hard to get where I am, and I am not going to let anyone keep me from getting what I want. Yes, ever once in a while I think about the great times back on Pleasant Street. I remember Mrs. Hill's bakery and Zeke the handyman, he taught us so many of the simpler things. Oh well, that's in the past, simpler days, simpler times. I must help make tomorrow better.

That's what I am here for… isn't it?

Spring

Spring and Other Things to Come, dedicated to my father Paul Young Carter May 03, 1915—April 20, 1996

SPRING—WHEN A YOUNG man's and a young lady's thoughts turn towards love.

You wouldn't know to look at him now, but once my dad was tall and strong. A disease known as Parkinson's has robbed him of much, but he is still my dad.

Spring reminds me of dogwood, its blossoms and when my dad was tall and strong.

I was fifteen, soon to be sixteen, and that winter I met a boy. Not just any boy, a boy that liked me as I liked him. He was my quintessential first love; he made me feel beautiful and special. We would go to movies and parties, talk for hours on the phone. When he would show up at the door or call on the phone dad would inform me in a voice full of disdain "It's that boy again". Dad, it seemed at the time, would listen briefly as I extolled *that boys'* virtues to Mom. Mom, as all mothers are, was thrilled when her daughter found a nice boy for her first boyfriend. I remember her telling dad when I wasn't supposed to be listening, "He's a good boy, from a good family. He treats her right, is respectful to us and always has her home on time." Dad just glared at his paper, noisily turning the pages, never uttering a word; yet his actions and silence spoke loudly.

Spring was coming, all fresh, budding and new. Everything was right with my world.

Saturday morning came. Dad was to gather dogwood blossoms for Mom's Sunday church group's tables.

I remember the look of helplessness on Dad's face as he returned from the mailbox and handed me my letter. The perfect boy had written to me. He wrote to tell me that he had found his true love. It was not to be me. I cried all morning, Dad puttered in the garage.

About noon Dad rapped on my bedroom door. He wanted me to help him go find, in his words, "Those dang blossoms." for Mom. We hunted and searched over back roads and hills.

Tramped for hours in the fresh smelling woods, finding just the right mix of pink and white for Mom.

Dad never asked, Dad never said I told you so. Dad just showed me that life did go on and no matter what; there was still one guy who thought I was beautiful and special.

Other Things to Come

A YEAR THIS spring, I wrote as an assignment for our writer's workshop about my first love, my first heartbreak, and how my dad got me through the pain of both.

Yesterday while watching my oldest son, I was given a glimpse of future things to come. A future where I may be expected to be as strong as my dad was that day long ago.

My son is a jock, a sports nut, a person who tells the seasons not by fall, winter, spring or summer, but by football, basketball, and baseball. He is twelve, tall and lanky. The top of his head is just past the shoulder of my own five-foot, six-inch frame. His favorite form of dress permits him to be a billboard of sorts for Bulls, Dawgs (yes, that's spelled D-A-W-G-S not D-O-G-S) and Thunder Birds. Creatures that constantly filled his mind excluding all else, or so I thought…until yesterday.

His baseball teammates and he were at practice. The boys, or should I say *young men,* haphazardly threw baseballs to each other and took their turn with the bat. All the while good-naturedly heckling each other's performances.

I sat quietly dividing my attention between the practice and a good book, when I became aware the atmosphere of light-heartedness had evaporated.

The boys, or young men, now were more serious, a seriousness usually reserved for real game time, not for a mere practice. There was something else now here. The air was charged with an electricity not associated with the sport, or at least the type of baseball I have grown accustom to these past four years.

A quick visual sweep of the area revealed the cause of the sudden change to the atmospheric conditions. To the untrained eye, they appeared harmless enough standing by one of the dugouts. Bright shining eyes, and small white teeth flashing, as soft excited sounds emanated from them. Their number totaled only four. There were twelve young men practicing on that field of green, but they were woefully outnumbered that day.

Because *The Four* were practicing for a game, a game much more ancient than that of baseball. A game with no real winners or losers but marked with casualties just the same.

The Four… were… girls, young women, and whereas it may not be one of these four in times to come, they were the first. They had caught my son's eye. They and their kind were now in his world.

They were now in my world, too.

I can only hope, when the time comes, and I have no doubt it will come. I can find a little piece of my dad's strength from that day long ago in me. Maybe I too can help soothe the pain of a broken heart over a first love as my dad did for me.

VAMPIRES

La Dernière Carte (The Last Card)

THE DREAMS WERE back with a vengeance, and clarity. They'd started a week before the anniversary of her mother, Penella, and grandmother, Tshilaba's deaths. Night after night, these women appeared in her dreams and spoke to her, but their words were garbled. As Josette reached out to them, their fingers nearly brushing hers, he would materialize. Tall with the Tarczal's dark handsome looks, his long stride bringing him toward her, his scent musky, tangy, and all things masculine. Her toes would curl, her stomach would quiver, her breasts would rise and fall. But before he reached her, she'd wake, her body aching and covered in sweat, leaving her wishing for the touch, taste, and sight of him.

The year was,1733 and it was the fifteenth

anniversary of her mother and grandmother's deaths and as the day neared its end, night pulled strongly at Josette. She hurried to gather the tools of her craft then stepped from her warm wagon into the dark.

A hulking shadow emerged from the night startling her. She strangled back a gasp. "Uncle, what are you doing here?"

"Everyone in the camp has noted your restlessness, and we fear for you. We've been keeping watch on you. You venture out on this night?"

"I must, Uncle." Family in the gypsy world didn't always mean a blood relative. The tribe adopted Josette after her mother and grandmother died in a wagon accident. The adoption blessed her with many extra uncles, aunts, and cousins.

"But the moon is tinged red tonight, and there have been sightings of a blood drinker in the area. What is so important that it draws you out on this night? Tell me it isn't just for coin."

"Coin would not be enough to lure me from our warm *Vardo*. No, a strong feeling and the cards dictate I leave the safety of the wagon and tribe."

They all knew of her gift; at times like this it was burden.

"I'll have Boldo accompany you."

"The king's son has better things to do than trail after one such as me." Josette didn't want Boldo shadowing her. He stank too much of wine and the cheap perfume of women not of the tribe. Besides, he was too free with his hands on her body. Her stomach rolled at the thought of his touch.

"I'll be fine. The walk isn't that far, and most villagers are home or huddled around the warm fire of a tavern."

The old man touched her shoulder. "Be careful, listen, and watch for shadows that would follow you."

"I will." She stood on tiptoe to kiss his withered cheek and was off.

Josette Cenehard Jovialis knew the Vieux Carré, or French Quarter, to outsiders, of New Orleans all too well. She'd been raised here since she was a tiny bundle. But as she made her way down a narrow street, for the first time in her life, the cold finger of fear caressed her spine. As with all the Cenehard women of the Machavaya gypsy tribe back until the dawn of time, Josette had been granted a sacrosanct gift. The *gift,* this magic that she usually donned, like a comforting, well-worn cloak, now quivered as if threatening to slide from her in a feeble attempt to flee. The gift couldn't escape her any more than she could escape it. Walking on, she did not quicken her step or look behind her. She raised her chin and strode forward along the street as the night silently stalked her.

The wind lifted the soft mass of caramel hued curls from her shoulders, as they spilled down her back. The color dispelled any rumors of her heritage being *Rom* or at the very least, *poshrat*. Her father, a tall man with reddish-blonde hair, spoke a foreign language unknown to her mother's tribe. While searching for herbs early one morning, her mother found him broken and bleeding. She mended him to the best of her abilities. That night he whispered his strange words to her mother bespelling her, according to the elders, and lay with her. When the next day broke, he was gone and her mother was with child. The tribe's elders, by the rules set down by their people, banished her mother and grand-mother, but the women soon found another tribe of Machavaya gypsies who eagerly welcomed them.

Josette tugged at her scarf, bringing it lower on the crown of her head. The good luck coins from her grandmother sewn along the front fold hid eyebrows that matched the curls in color. A blouse the tint of dried blood pulled tight across a well-rounded form. It dipped low on milky shoulders that peeked from beneath a strikingly patterned silk shawl. A long leather waist-cinch girdled slender hips over a skirt of heavy, dark silks. Boots, buttery soft, encased long slim legs. Her delphinium-blue eyes, slanted cat-like at their corners, inspected the gloom, as if she thought to actually see what stalked her. Each step was accented by the jingle of long, exotic earrings and the jangle of her many bracelets.

Covering her mouth and nose with a many-times mended lace handkerchief, she attempted to block out the over ripe malodors. She stepped over garbage strewn along building sides and puddles from the morning's downpour. Down one shadow-infested street then another she made her way. She startled once when a grimalkin jumped from the shadows to chase a fat rodent. As she drew closer to the tavern, she could hear the boisterous, jubilant sounds emanating from beyond its door. The night slipped silently along, behind her, devouring the shapes of all it touched, changing itself into one form after another.

Now, she quickened her stride to the Bloody Boar Tavern. Reaching for the latch, she jumped back as the door burst outward. Three patrons, two holding up the third, staggered into the night. The trio reeked of ale and cheap perfume from the women or woman they'd been with. They never saw her or her distress as they stumbled away. Under her breath she scolded herself and told her racing heart to calm itself, then entered the tavern. Unwashed bodies packed together for warmth and comfort. Meat cooking, yeasty ale and the oil from the lamps assaulted her nose. As her eyes adjusted to the dim, smoky interior, she pulled off her shawl and nodded to a few familiar faces.

She made her way to her regular table at the back of the room. She took the medium-sized pouch with its doeskin strap from her shoulder and reverently removed several items, placing them on the highly polished table before her. As she had been taught, she prepared the space and in doing so honored those before her. One by one, she arranged four candles, green to the north, red to the south, clear yellow to the east, and dark blue to the west. In the center of the candles, she placed a tiny silver dish where she sprinkled a bit of tansis root and sandalwood, igniting them.

Watching her, the myriad of *gaujos*, her would-be customers respectfully hung back. They waited for her to finish the ritual *dukkerin* before approaching with their pieces of silver. She believed her grandmother to be a true *shuvani*, and like her, Josette felt as one with the cards. She withdrew the dog-eared yet—still exquisite cards from their sanctuary, shuffled them, and began the pattern of placement. When all was ready, she positioned her hands with palms up on the table, leaned back, closing her eyes, and willed her mind to clear and her body to relax. Opening her eyes she reached to turn the first card and found her hand hesitated with a hair's-breadth above it before turning over the card. The watchful patrons did not miss the hesitation. One by one she unveiled each card and deciphered its meaning. Her delicate, translucent, heart-shaped face became paler as she revealed each card. The last card loomed before her. She swallowed hard as she reached for it then gasped as a large, callused hand covered hers.

"You tremble, gypsy. Why, when you are so intimate with the cards' secret, do you fear the last one?"

The man from her dreams stood before her, a Tarczal, a drinker of blood. He smiled at her. Blue-black hair pulled back into a neatly formal queue glowed in the lamplight and framed off a face chiseled and marred. A patch covered his left eye and a small portion of the jagged scar that dipped sharp into the cheek. The lone eye, whose gaze now bore deep into her, was a ghostly blue gray.

"I fear not their truths, and certainly not any *mere* man." She'd recognized members of his ancient race in the quarter before, no doubt hunting their next meal. They called themselves Tarczal after the mountains where they and her tribe originated. This was the first time she'd been this close to one, and her heartbeat like a rabbit's. Her hand tingled under his, but she would not give him the satisfaction of being the first to pull away. Still, there was the matter of the last card to be turned.

HE NEARLY GRINNED at her attempt to put him in his place but quelled the reflex. Never moving his hand from hers, he reached out with his free hand to draw a chair near to him and promptly straddled it.

"Bold talk for someone whose trembling I feel even as we speak, but perhaps it is not from fear at all but from the cold," He gestured with his hand. "There is a slight draft in here." Then leaning across the table closer to her, said, "Or perhaps it is only the nearness of *my* presence that makes you tremble and your heart race." He watched, mesmerized, as the pulse in her neck scurried along its path. Consequently, he was caught off guard as her free hand connected solidly with his cheek, nearly unseating him.

Many in the tavern had ceased their drinking, gambling, and whoring to watch the pair and now from deep in the crowd someone snickered.

The Tarczal, what the blood drinkers called themselves, straightened slowly. His gaze and hers locked.

SOMETHING DARK FLICKERED behind his eye and for a moment Josette feared him. Then the *something* slid away and the smile that he quelled before now spread broadly across his face. To her amazement, he threw back his head and laughed loudly. "Well done little catamount, few, very few have dared to attack me and even fewer have *lived* to tell of it."

Her eyes narrowed. "I did not attack first. I only choose to defend myself… and I will do so again if I must." She could not believe her boldness. Her good sense made her discreetly feel through the slit in her skirt pocket for the dagger strapped to her thigh, though she knew its presence was false comfort. The corner of his mouth twitched in annoyance or amusement. She did not know which, as he considered her words. Gently he withdrew his hand from atop hers. Raising one eyebrow he glanced down at the last card before returning his gaze to her.

Even before she turned the card over, she knew its name.

With the deftness from years of practice, she turned the card over and the people crowding around her lost their collective breath. A skeletal Dragon boldly hung in the murkiness and mist of the Netherworld. A scythe grasped in one hand. Death.

The stranger appeared nonplused.

"An interesting card is it not, gypsy?"

"It is a card misinterpreted by many who do not understand its meaning," she coolly replied.

"So, tell me soothsayer, what does it mean tonight?"

Josette quelled herself from shifting nervously in her seat, "The card represents death. But death—be it of the flesh or thought—can mean change and not necessarily a loss."

"Forgive me, but isn't change, a loss in itself?"

"Well yes, what I was referring to was, the loss of perhaps a loved one."

"A loved one, but you also mentioned the loss of thought."

"I... sir you seek to twist my words, even confuse me. To what purpose do you do this?"

"I only asked a question and then made an observation. Do you fear something gypsy?"

"As I have stated I certainly do not fear you sir."

"I should hope not, precious one." His voice had gone low, sensual, and honeyed, as though they were alone in the room. Then with a small upward tilt of his chin, his voice returned to its previous timber. "This loss or change could perchance mean the loss of love for oneself?"

"That would be..." Josette struggled with the words. Afraid her reply would be the answer he wanted and one that she did not wish to face. "...a possibility."

"Whom did you draw these cards for, gypsy? No one in particular...or did you? Perhaps you drew them with a question of your *own* in mind?"

"I asked no question... they were drawn for... I drew them because..."

"Who, Josette, who do the cards speak for

tonight?"

"I…" How did he know her name? Even the owner and the patrons of the bar did not know it. They had always referred to her as the gypsy.

A large shadow drifted over the table where they sat. The barkeep, who now stood very near the stranger's shoulder, held a large brawl-breaker, a night-man's stick, in his beefy hands. "Here now, don't be deviling our gypsy. You've taken up enough of her time and there's other *paying* patrons here who want a turn." A small rumble of voices acknowledged the innkeeper's words.

"I have paid for a reading." Later, all would swear later that before the stranger noted its presence, that no coin…of any value…had previously laid there.

The bartender and many of the patrons shifted uncomfortably.

"And you shall receive a reading, sir." Josette gathered up the cards and began to shuffle the cards and lay them out.

After a slight nod from Josette assuring him, all was well, the bartender ambled back to tending his taps.

The spread revealed the usual or that is what *she* relayed to the Tarczal. Wealth would cross his path, and if he were observant, he could reap its benefits. A battle for power would be his for the winning if he believed in his own strength of character. And finally, should he be receptive to Creiddylad and praise her, love would come to him willingly.

"Lucky in wealth, power… and love. All I have to do is open my eyes and want what is offered. A most enlightened reading, thank you, Mademoiselle." The stranger rose from his seat much to everyone's surprise, bowed to her and strolled over to the bar. For the rest of the evening, he stayed there, sometimes just standing there watching her, nursing his mead.

NICLAYS CHÂTILLON PONDERED the situation. It was obvious no one had told Josette of their impending marriage. She knew nothing of him, which meant the connection hadn't been completed. What was he to do? Time was running out. He was forbidden from telling her any more than that they were to be married, or the spell wouldn't be lifted. Could he make her fall in love with him? He'd dreamed of her every night and fantasized about each and every curve on her. The woman in the flesh made those images laughable.

It gladdened him and saddened him. He was but a poor excuse of a man to be offering himself as a husband to one who could be a queen. Perhaps it would be better if he slunk off to die and left her alone. But therein lay the rub; he couldn't bring himself to leave her.

Niclays knew the entire story of how they became betrothed. His sire and grandsire whose lineage was as muddy as a stream after storm, learned how to breed back true to the Tarczal race of their ancestors. The crux of the curse was that Josette must fall in love with him on her own and be willing to take him to her bed and surrender her heart, body, and soul to him.

As the hour grew late, and the patrons stumbled out Niclays thought it best to wait for Josette outside; alone he might be able to seduce her. He slipped out the door unnoticed.

JOSETTE WENT ABOUT her business reading cards or palms, whichever the customer preferred. The evening went well other than one incident. A patron with too much drink in him didn't like his reading. He'd become belligerent about it until someone offered to buy him another drink. Then he'd stumbled off mumbling about cards, gypsies, and nonsense. All in all, it was a brisk evening for Josette. She did her best to ignore the stranger with the eye patch at the bar. For brief periods she was able to block him from her mind. That was until she raised her head and glimpsed him through the milling crowd. He'd smiled and raised his tankard in salute, or sometimes just wink. The latter infuriated Josette but long ago she'd learned to school her features. She found it was better not to give anything away to customers. Or those around her.

The hour was late, and most customers had wandered home or to somewhere they could sleep off the effects of the drink. Some would be lucky, partially due to her readings, and find themselves in a warm bed with a willing partner. Josette found it was always good to notice who was admiring whom and use it to her advantage.

Josette gathered her things, placed them back safely in her bag and donned her shawl, adjusting it on her shoulders. She braced herself, expecting to be placed in the position of warding off the advances of the stranger. But he was nowhere in sight. She gave the barkeep his share of the night's take. He in return gave her a small sack with bread, cheese, a bit of meat, and a flagon of mead.

An arrangement they had struck long ago. She clutched the sack and stepped out into the night's fog.

A gust, grave-chilled crept around her ankles, slid up her legs, burrowed itself under her skirts. It climbed up her thighs around her waist to painfully grip her shoulders. She pulled her shawl tighter around her and clutched the sack closer. The same gust left her to wrestle and roll with fallen leaves. It tossed them up, twisting swirling to send dark shapes scurrying from their hiding places.

And then she heard them.

Footsteps echoing hers.

When Josette stopped, the other stopped. So, she thought ruefully, the stranger had waited for her. As she carefully moved onward, she retrieved her hidden dagger.

Down one street and across another she went, the footfalls moving when she did, stopping as she did. It was not the first time someone had followed her, hoping to steal her purse or something more personal. Josette hurried down one alley and slipped between loose boards in the fence at the end. A twist here and a turn there and she paused in a doorway to listen. She hadn't heard any footsteps since the alley where she given him the slip. She smiled to herself. Once again, the trick had worked. Josette slipped her dagger back into its hiding place. Briskly she stepped from her back into the alley. Because she was straightening her shawl, which had come askew in her haste, she did not see the man that stepped in front of her.

"Thieving gypsy, takin a man's hard-earned money and only givin' him a pretty word or two in return. A man needs more than that." Catching her off guard he roughly shoved her against the building, pinning her by the forearms.

Josette's head snapped back colliding with the brick wall, dazing her. The only thing keeping her standing was the man's body now pressed against hers.

"Just a kiss for ole Mick." Dully, Josette was aware of his mouth on hers. He stank of ale, sweat, and decaying teeth. Josette gagged at the stench and turned her head trying to avoid him.

"So you gots a little fight in ya. Ole Mick likes 'em when they gots some life in 'em." His hands began to wander over her as he pressed his body even closer to her. Still dazed Josette fought to find the strength to push him away from her.

The last turn was when he'd lost her, he was sure of it, and now he was retracing his steps. Niclays paused, searching the alley for a clue as to which way she'd gone. She was a crafty one, he'd give her that. He hoped, as a member of the house of Châtillon, he would in the end be more cunning. He was about to turn and leave when something shiny caught his eye near the fence blocking the alley's end. Niclays retrieved it and held it up for a closer look. The moonlight skittered off the article in his hand, a gold coin with a tiny hole near its top. It was one of the many that had adorned Josette's headpiece. As he began to straighten up a board slightly awry in the fence drew his attention. He pushed on it and stepped through the opening.

Josette brought her knee up sharply hoping to connect with the man's groin, but he was an old dog, wise to many a trick. "Now what for you go do'in that? Ol'Mick ain't wanti'in to hurt ya. I's just want'in some of your sweetness."

Niclays had nearly reached the alley's end

when a muffled scream and the renting of material reached his ears. Like an enraged bull, Niclays rounded the corner, saw the man and grabbed him by the scruff of his neck. He tossed the drunkard aside as if he were a bad piece of meat not even fit for dogs. The wretch landed in a heap several feet away and lay there. Niclays did not see or care where the man ended up; his only concern was for Josette.

HER SCARF AND hair had covered her face as she'd struggled with the man. Josette was disorientated from the blow and blinded by her scarf. Thinking she was only momentarily freed from the drunk, she franticly reached her dagger.

IN HIS RELIEF to see she was not badly harmed, Niclays grasped her by the shoulders, pulling her to him.

There was a flash of steel.

Only blind instinct saved his life.

"By the Goddess woman." Niclays dabbed at the shallow but profusely bleeding wound with his fingertips. "'If you'd had any skill with that thing, I might be seriously injured. And you'd be a widow before you're wed."

Josette pushed the hair and scarf from her eyes to find the stranger from the tavern before her.

"Who are you, sir? Why do you persist in following me?"

He tried to bow, grimaced, and then smiled at her. "Niclays of the house of Châtillon. Your betrothed and very soon to be husband for I've grown tired of a cold bed."

Betrothed? Soon to be husband? This was all too much. Those were Josette's last thoughts before her mind slipped blissfully into darkness.

IN THE SOFT candlelight, Niclays checked his bandaged side and frowned at the stained cloth… and the situation. The night had not gone at all as he had hoped or planned. At least Josette hadn't been repulsed by his face as he'd feared she might. Or if she had been, hid it well. His fist clenched revealing a sudden unguarded moment of anger. By the Goddess, she was beautiful. He watched her sleep. She was so young or maybe he just felt too old. Feet propped up, arms crossed over his chest Niclays' head slowly drooped. He slept soundly.

HER GRANDMOTHER TSHILABA'S voice whispered in her head as the first soft golden rays of light tiptoed through the poorly shuttered windows. *Help him. Save him. Love him.* Josette woke with a dull but bearable headache. Cautiously, she opened her eyes to check out her surroundings and her gaze rested on him. He slept still seated in the chair, softly snoring, not an unpleasant sound, more reassuring and comforting. Under the blanket, she still wore her clothes save for her boots. She'd not been touched. He'd protected her when he could have… startled she remembered his words to her. They were betrothed. How?

Her thoughts were interrupted by footfalls in the hallway and a sharp rap at the door. Niclays woke, stretched lazily, saw that she, too, was awake and smiled slowly, seductively. Then he rose to answer the door.

"Bonjour, Monsieur, I bring the meal you requested last night." The girl's smile faltered when she noticed Josette lying on the bed. Niclays frowned, realizing the girl had hoped to share the meal and perhaps more with him. It appeared he could attract any woman except the one he wanted.

"Merci, Mimet. Be so good as to leave it on the table."

The girl laid the tray down and snubbing Josette, turned to him. "Will there be anything else, Monsieur?"

"Oui, tell your mistress I'll need clean towels, hot water and her best scented soap. I'm sure, the Mademoiselle will want to refresh herself." He pressed several coins into the girl's hand. "And Mimet, keep any coin not needed for the payment for yourself."

"Oui Monsieur, merci, Monsieur." Her eyes widened at the extra amount of coin she held as Niclays gently nudged her towards the door and finally out into the hallway. He stepped over to the table, lifting one lid after another inspecting the dishes. "I ordered your eggs poached, a bit of porridge, bread toasted and a pot of dark tea with honey. If you require anything else tell me and I will have it brought to you." The night hadn't gone as planned, but he was glad he'd thought to place the order before leaving last night.

Josette stared at him, puzzled. "Why are you

being so…kind, sir?"

Kind. He let the word echo in his mind. It was not something many had ever called him. He knew she was waiting for an answer and found himself stalling. Lifting one last lid, he raised an eyebrow; the serving girl had included fresh berries and a pitcher of cream. Good thing he'd tipped her well in advance, he could ill afford a jealous retribution on her part. He turned back to Josette who was now delicately pouring a cup of tea.

"Feeding you is not an act of kindness. But one of necesity. I cannot have my fiancée expiring from lack of nourishment. Especially after your ordeal of last night. How are you feeling?"

Josette set her cup of tea down and gingerly pressed her fingertips to the back of her head. "I feel fine and hungry. The eggs do look good."

Niclays watched her anxiously. "I saw no breaking of the skin or blood. Nevertheless, I placed a cooling herb compress over the bump."

"I'm well enough, sir. There is plenty here, won't you join me?" She wished to draw the conversation away from herself.

He could understand that desire. He picked up a berry, popped it in his mouth and leaned over her. Josette thought he was going to kiss her and found she wanted his mouth, his touch on her.

"Would you like fresh berries and cream on your porridge?" He nudged a berry against her mouth and as her lips parted popped it in. Because he wanted to kiss her, he popped one in his own mouth, too.

"Mmmmmm, these are very good, don't you agree?"

JOSETTE CHEWED THE berry, savoring its flesh and juices as she studied him and chose her words carefully. "Yes, they are delicious, all of this," she waved her hand towards the tray, "has been delightful and I thank you for it as well as your kindness. But…I feel you do this under a mistaken impression. I am not yours or anyone's fiancée."

Niclays eased back in his chair and stretched his legs out before him. "I am not mistaken Josette. You *are* to be mine."

He noted with some curiosity that she revealed nothing of her thought or emotion at his pronouncement. "Did your mother, Penella, or grandmother, Tshilaba, not tell you I would one day come for you?

She placed her hands in her lap head bowed. "My mother and grand both died many years ago in a carriage accident."

"How many years?"

"I was a child of five."

"How old are you now?"

"Twenty and one, sir."

"Their accident happened before they could tell you of the pact."

"No one told me of any pact, least of all a pact concerning my betrothal to one such as you, sir."

"Save your family and mine, no one else knew of this promise. Nevertheless, we are promised to each other, and I have tasted your blood, which sealed the concordat."

Her hand flew to her neck.

"Not recently, my love, when you were but a toddler a drop or two of your blood was shared with me."

"By whom?" she snapped.

"Your mother and grandmother."

Josette tried to hide her dismay at this news. Her hands plucking at her skirt gave her away. Why had the two women she trusted above all else shared her blood with this Tarczal? Niclays shifted in his seat, and she noticed the blood stain on his tunic from last night was still wet.

"Why isn't your wound healing? Your kind is known for their swift regenerative abilities."

"I'm different from my brethren."

"How?"

"The pact prevents me from divulging that information."

A clatter of horse hooves on the cobblestones echoed off the store and home fronts culminating in a deafening crescendo below their window. Niclays strode to the window and peered out cautiously. A group of twenty gendarmerie waited outside while their captain, no doubt, was already inside the inn.

"What's going on?"

"Shush…" Niclays cracked open the window to listen to the men below. It took but a minute for him to hear all he needed. "Get your boots on…" he snapped then turned to see Josette already finishing up the laces.

"Can you cross the rooftops?" He pushed the large wardrobe in front of the door.

"Of course, but I'm not leaving until you tell me why."

"There is no time to explain…" he stopped, shook his head as she firmly planted her feet with arms crossed under her breasts, giving him a delectable view of the ample mounds.

He pulled her towards the window as he explained. "Someone broke into the bar where you read the cards last night and beat the bartender to death. They found a tarot card clenched in his fist and his money box gone."

"Oh, no."

The sound of angry voices and many boots coming up the stairs forced Niclays into action. He pushed and pulled Josette to the open window. Securing Josette around the waist with one arm, he used his other arm to swing her to the adjacent roof top before joining her. He clasped her hand in his, and they began quickly to walk the roof's spine to the next building.

"Why are we running?"

"Who do you think they believe killed the bartender?"

"Us? Why on earth?"

"Your card. My strength."

"Oh, but we didn't…"

"We know that they don't. Keep moving."

"We have to explain…"

"I don't believe they're in the mood to listen. Besides who's going to believe a rogue half-breed Tarczal and a gypsy?"

Josette shook her head in resignation and kept

walking along the rooftops.

Thwack! A musket ball slammed into a roof tile exploding it into a thousand pieces. Niclays grabbed Josette, drawing her to him his body shielding her. Thwack! Thwack! More tiles disintegrated around them.

"There, over there. See it, the open window?"

Josette nodded.

"Run!"

Hot. Burning. Pain. Rolled over him. Niclays glanced down to see blood soaking his tunic. Instead of running, Josette stood frozen. He snatched her to him, his mouth hungry for her. The kiss was deep, hot, and finished in an instant. "Run." He said standing between her and the next volley. "Run." He shoved her in the direction of the gaping window. "I love you, now run damn it, run!"

Josette scrambled down the roof sliding to the window and as she popped inside safely for the moment Niclays fell backwards into the air.

JOSETTE GASPED AS she reached out her hand to him in spite of the distance and then watched as he disappeared from her sight. His words, "I love you" and "run" echoed in her mind. Ducking inside the opening, she eyed the door and froze when she saw the couple on the bed. Engrossed in their bouncing, they didn't notice her hurry across the room to slip out the door.

Down the stairs she rushed, pulling her shawl high and her scarf low before pausing at the bottom. She glanced around the room and located the back door. She hastened out into an alleyway, assessed her safety and to her relief, not only did no one follow her, but she realized she knew this area. Josette sped toward a little used barn. Her knees shook, and Josette sat hard on the hay piled high on the floor behind her. When she brought her fist to her mouth to stifle a sob, she tasted blood. Josette held out her hand turned it over and saw the back was smeared with Niclays blood. She expected to be revolted by what she was about to do. Instead, it seemed natural. Remembering his words about him tasting her blood, she licked one finger clean.

Bursts of light danced before her eyes. When she blinked them away, an image of Niclays young and whole appeared. Another likeness sprang to replace the first, this time Niclays as she knew him now, older married and determined. This image stood in the barn with her. It faded as fast as the first image, leaving her alone.

She could hide there, undetected until she found out if Niclays lived or died. It didn't take long to find the answer to that question the village buzzed with the news. Josette had placed the white scrap of her petticoat in the broken window, a sign to her tribe, a member was inside and needed help. Her plight would be known to her people quickly enough someone would see the sign. It wasn't long before a young boy of seven slipped into the barn with a canteen of water, instructions to lead her back to the camp, and the information she needed. Niclays lived, but only until morning when he'd face a firing squad.

"BOLDO PLEASE, TWO horses that's all I need."

Boldo, stood arms crossed, brow furrowed. "You will bring the police here with this crazy plan. Do you know what they will do to us? They will drive us from the area or worse burn our wagons and kill those who are too slow or feeble to escape. All for a blood drinker."

"You summoned me back here. Someone killed the tavern owner, and the blame has fallen on the Tarczal and me. He helped me flee the police. I must help him."

"If I aid you, you must promise yourself to me. My father, the king, never approved the blood drinker's 'pact'.

Josette stepped back, her gaze locking with Boldo's. "How do you know of the agreement? I only found out yesterday."

Boldo's eyes narrowed. "You *will* be mine. My father was a fool for letting your mother and grandmother form that pact with the *guyos*. You and your magic are mine." He shot out his arm grabbing her wrist, pulling her to him. Josette winced from his grip. But his hand slipped from its hold on her. She watched as Boldo crumpled to the ground, unconscious exposing two of her gypsy uncles, Gudada and Marko.

"Now we know who made it seem that you and the Tarczal murdered the innkeeper."

"Hurry! There isn't much time." They hustled her to where three horses stood waiting.

"Why are you helping me?"

"The tribe knew this day would come. The seer told us we must aid you and the Tarczal. He's guarded us for many years, and it's time we repaid his protection."

"I don't understand."

"You will soon enough, child." The uncles

assisted her onto one horse and mounted the other two. "Gudada knows where in the jail they're keeping him. We'll get him out and then it will be up to you to take him as far from here as possible."

The Gypsy Cobs they rode made fast the distance from the glen outside the city to the jailhouse deep inside the town's center. Their feathered legs muffled the sound of their hooves on the cobble stones.

Gudada and Marko tied ropes from their saddles to the bars of the jail's window; with a shout, the men urged the horses forward. The strong draft style animals drew the lines tight; the stone and mortar groaned, shuddered, and for a moment held strong. Powerful hooves dug into the ground as the horses threw themselves against the bindings, and the wall crumbled into dust.

Gudada and Marko released the lines from their steeds and hurried into the cell. Moments later they stumbled out with Niclays between them, half conscious, and hoisted him across the saddle in front of Josette.

"Go child! Ride fast and true. Find a safe place at the foot of the mountain."

"But what of you and the tribe?"

Shouts and sharp whistles sounded the alarm.

"By now the wagons are deep in the forest, and as its night the gendarmerie will be unable to find us."

"Will I ever see you again?"

"We will find each other when the time is right. Now go!" And with that Marko slapped her horse's rump and they flew down the avenues.

The horse glided down the streets with a mind of its own. Josette let the animal have its head and did her best to keep Niclays body across the horse's neck. They plunged from the city's light to the safety of darkness, and still the animal followed a path only it knew.

By morning's first rays, they were far from the town and those who would hunt them. They needed shelter and rest. Josette sat scanning the area for any refuge and spied a cave opening that was nearly hidden from sight. The horse sensed where she wanted to go and hastened to the cave. Josette dismounted, lit a torch, and led them deep into the fissure. There she found fresh water and a dry, raised spot where after lining it with the furs the uncles had provided, she wrestled Niclays off the saddle.

NICLAYS DREAMED OF a soft bed and a softer woman. He dreamed of a life with the woman, a simple life filled with love, laughter, and children. Boys with his dark looks and girls beautiful like their mother. A wave of pain rolled over him, his body cramped and twitched from the loss of blood. Niclays fought the darkness that called to him. He must see her one more time. He opened his eyes to the torch light and the small fire designed to warm him, yet he felt no heat, only the cold of death trying to claim him.

"Josette?"

"Niclays, you're awake. I've done all I know how to do, but I can't stop the bleeding. Tell me what to do." She'd taken off his blood-soaked clothing and washed him before attempting to bandage his wound.

"Shush, there is nothing you can do to stop it."

"There must be something."

"Come closer my love; give me one kiss, my sweet, my only one. Let me know the taste of your light and goodness, even so briefly."

"Oh, Niclays." Josette leaned down, her lips brushed his, but he wanted more.

"Lay with me Josette. Let me know the joy of you pressed close to me."

She stood and made quick the dropping of her skirt and pulling her blouse over her head, the pouch holding her runes and cards tumbled to the edge of the stone platform. Josette lay down along his length. Her lips found his again. As Niclays placed his hand on the nap of her neck, desire ignited in his gut and spread warmth from his head to toes. As quickly as it flared, the gray of death snuffed it out and Niclays hand fell to his side.

THE KISS THRILLED and intoxicated her. Her fingers sought to soothe and entice his fevered flesh. A chill threatened to steal the heat from his body. If she didn't act with haste, he would leave this world. She rose to place her candles, one at his head, one at his feet, and one each on either side of him. Lighting each, she gave a blessing to the goddess and all that was sacred to the Mother. Earlier she'd ground herbs found growing outside the cave, and now she sprinkled them on his forehead and chest.

"Hear me Mother to all whose breath, give life to the world,

I come before you, one of your children.

I am small and weak.

Your strength and wisdom are sought to heal this warrior.

Take all that I am as a sacrifice to heal this man.

Take the power granted to the Machavaya women who walked before me

Hear my plea, take my life, my energy and give it to this warrior.

He is a warrior of strength, kindness, and all that is good.

Breathe your gift into his cooling body, bring fire back to him.

So mote it be."

Josette knelt beside him. A tear slid down her cheek and splashed onto his chest as she leaned over to kiss his lips.

IN THE DISTANCE Niclays heard her plea, felt her tear upon his flesh, and then the gentle press of her mouth to his. Warmth spread from that touch, down his body, and as strength sprang into him the wound at his side began to close. He stretched his arm to pull her down, the length her body, sweet and willing, covered his. Niclays deepened the kiss, reveling in the honey of her, the silkiness of her skin and hair, and inhaled the scent that was hers alone. In one swift movement, he rolled her onto her back switching their positions.

"My Josette, I've dreamed of hold you so, making love to you 'til our bodies are spent from desire." He plundered her mouth, nipping at her lips, swirling his tongue with hers. Niclays groaned with delight when her hands caressed his chest. He kissed her face, and neck, whispering Tarczal words of love.

"Let me make you mine even for this one brief time before the goddess takes me from your light." The sound of water dripping into the cave's basin ticked off the moments.

She leaned up to kiss his lips, her hands exploring every inch of him. "Yes, I too have dreamed, of you Niclays, make us one."

He drew her to him and continued kissing her as he ran his hands up and down her back. Josette nibbled along his jaw then ran the tip of her tongue over the shell of his ear. She played with the springy hair covering his chest. Josette arched her back, tangling her fingers in Niclays' ebony hair and snapping the leather tie that held it back.

She kissed his chest.

He kissed the tip of her nose, "Oh, Niclays don't stop." She sighed. against his mouth.

Later, Josette lay drowsily in his arms; he smiled brushing his mouth across the top of her head. "Sleepy?" he whispered.

A contented, hmmmmm, was her answer and then she opened her eyes and with an ear-splitting squeal shouted, "Your face, your eye!"

"I'm sorry I wasn't thinking." He started to search for the patch that hid his disfigurement.

Josette sat up to take his face in her hands. "No, Niclays look at me, look…at…me."

"I…" he shot his hand to his face, the flesh, once puckered and scarred, was whole again. He blinked several times before realizing he did so with both eyes.

"The Goddess has healed you. She's blessed you and mended the wound at your side and wiped the damage from your face."

The Goddess had indeed changed him. He felt this new life coursing through him. A sharp ache of pain shot in his mouth, and his tongue explored teeth unique to his Tarczal heritage. Teeth hidden behind his upper front teeth, razor sharp able to puncture skin without causing pain so a Tarczal could obtain nourishment from another human. The pact was fulfilled, his body changed. He was now a fully-fledged Tarczal. That could only mean one thing.

"You love me?" His gaze locked on hers.

"Of course I do, from the moment you came to me in my dreams."

"Say them, say the words my heart longs to hear from your lips, my sweet."

"I love you, Niclays of the house of Châtillon, now and forever."

He reached his arm around her to pillow her head as he leaned in for a kiss. At the same time his elbow brushed the bag holding her tarot cards lying near his head. The pouch's opening parted, and a lone card slid out. It drifted first to the left then to the right to land face up, the last card finally revealed. The Lovers.

New Player in Town

I met a new vampire last night in my dreams and don't like him. He's too bold for my taste. He started out looking like Charles Shaughnessy from the show 'The Nanny', that's when he was leaning up against the wall of a building close by. I thought that was cute not that he was leaning against the building but that he looked like Charles Shaughnessy. But by the time he crossed the sidewalk and came halfway across the street to our table he had changed. Even now I can 'see' the memory of his face in my mind's eye, but when I try to focus on it, it blurs and I can't see enough to describe. I can safely say he has dark hair, thin, no, not thin, slender and the muscles are certainly smooth, defined and strong. Very strong. We, my husband and I, were at a festival of some sorts and the streets had been closed off.

It was night. One street had rides, and I remember standing and watching one in particular and feeling queasy just watching it go through its motions. Another street had rows and rows of cafeteria tables and that's where we were sitting, across from Ed Bagley Jr. no less and as my husband was telling Ed about my work which Ed was familiar with (go figure?!) especially the zines work. I saw this vampire leaning against the building watching me.

Many people were dressed as characters from fiction. Oh there were gypsies and people on stilts dressed as clowns or colonial people but many, many were dressed as vampires. Men dressed in full tuxes or just black shirts and pants. Women with plunging necklines and handkerchief scarf hemmed skirts some made to appear as if they were old and tattered. The colors of the dresses varied from plain black to red and black and some almost gypsy-like with strong bright colors. Wild hair always black, pale to white makeup and of course the bloody mouths with the sharp pointed teeth. Funny now that I think of it and remember I'd thought the gems they wore at their ears, necks and on their hands to look surprisingly real. All those in costume danced and playfully scampered about smiling and mingling with the crowd that came to 'eat, drink, and be merry'.

I realize now they were hunting, singling out and picking their prey. These were real vampires playing at being vampires.

He came over to our table wearing the black tux, a black cape with red silk lining and on his hands, he wore white gloves. I remember the gloves because I can still feel how they felt as he took my hand then hands into his. I thought them an odd yet stereotypical accessory. "Every-one is dancing, come dance with me", he said and my husband and Ed laughed and said, "Vampire writer go dance with the vampire".

I was nervous, giddy, and knew something wasn't quite right.

First, he twirled me from one dance step to another taking me farther and farther away from where my husband sat. How odd I thought because I couldn't dance and yet the steps came so naturally to my feet. Then he pulled me against him drawing his cloak around both of us. Away from my husband, not too far as to arouse suspicion but far enough I couldn't make out where he sat. Up to another building and a bench that rested there, he pulled me down beside him and we sat, me cuddled in beside him, he had his arms around me the two of us looking for the rest of the world like lovers. It began to rain a fine mist, and someone stood beside him and held an umbrella over us. The umbrella was huge and blocked most of the outside view from me and me from it. He tried to kiss me, I felt uncomfortable and resisted, then he kissed me, hard, knowingly, thoroughly, and the uneasiness in my stomach grew to fear. When he pulled back and I saw his face the faint smile on his mouth as he stared down at me and his eyes, hungry with I don't know what stared at me I wanted to leave.

It stopped raining and the umbrella, and its holder, disappeared.

A woman flew overhead at a leisurely pace maybe at a height of ten feet cursing and alternating between shouting and muttering in a language I never heard but knew resembled those of the Slavic nations. Another woman strode from the sidewalk out into the street waving the fist of one hand into the air at the woman while her other hand clutched the shawl she wore around her shoulders tightly to her breast. She shouted in English something I can't remember now but know it was telling the flying woman to stop what she was doing, or the locals were going to catch on.

The flying woman landed and went about her

way, the shawl lady shook her head glanced at me, shifted her gaze to him and I felt him nodding. He was telling her with a single look I wasn't a threat. She nodded to him and turned to go about her own designs.

And then I woke up, or at least that's all I can recall at the moment.

With the hero of my vampire story, I've always felt safe but this man, this vampire, frightens me even now in the warm sunlight of morning.

I felt for a moment, now sitting here writing this, lucky to be awake and safe in my home and a horrible thought slammed into my head. I'm not safe, he'll come again, he's not finished with me.

He whispers in my head that when I call to my characters, telling me it only takes one time and he can keep my hero out forever, smiling all the while.

I'm afraid.

We Do Differ So

A PERFUME OF fresh scrubbed cleanness, an innocence of young womanhood, tantalized his senses. The wearer of this perfume was the epitome of an American Cheerleader, almost. Blond tresses fell to the small of a petite form's back. A clear complexion, but the face held not the customary blue eyes. Hers were an emerald, green.

"Excuse me, Miss?" his accent European and delightfully rich, vibrant. "I believe you dropped this."

She turned to find a gentleman tall and pale, hair of jet, and eyes of indigo behind her in the crowed store.

Her scarf, he held in his hand. "Why, thank you very much. This was a gift." She reached for the scarf not touching his hand with hers. "And I would have hated to have lost it," her voice soft and low, he strained to hear it.

His hand touched the scarf, lightly, revering. "It seems very old. The design reminds me of my homeland. An old Tarczal design I once knew well. Many outsiders mistake our mountains and culture with Transylvania. The two regions, in fact, border each other, but we do differ so." For a moment, his eyes looked beyond her. "The Tarczals are a proud people. Many have family histories they can date back several hundreds of years."

Shivering in the night air, as they had since left the shop, he once again turned his gaze back to her. "Forgive me sometimes I digress. The past is at times more present than…the…present."

Their path led them to the town's large downtown parking lot. "Your town looks so festive in its October Fest and Halloween decorations." Gazing up at the soft-lit courthouse steeples, he smiled like a delighted child. "Oh look! Even the bats collecting the night bugs seem so very much in place!"

Then as the courthouse clock announced the hour was at its half, he paused mid stride. "Why you must think me rude. Here, I, a stranger, have followed you and not even once given you my name. Vladamire Markrava, at your service madam." He bowed deeply, then as he rose, took her hand and brushed his lips across it like a butterfly's caress, kissed it.

She smiled a sweet smile. "Mr. Markrava, I am delighted to meet you. Please, tell me more about yourself." Taking his warm hand into her cool one, they continued their walk. Down many small streets to the town's park and Little League, ball fields. A light mist was settling over the cemetery just beyond both.

Vladamire Markrava continued to talk of his missed homeland and its colorful past. She listened eagerly to each word; her eyes now sparkled with a hungering anticipation.

"We have much in common, sir. My family was from Europe, too. They fled to America to escape persecution from others. Others, who feared what they did not know or understand," her voice shook with a tightly leashed anger.

He looked at her surprised. "You have no accent to your speech. I never would have known."

The darkness and evening shadows now hid her face.

"Yes, we have worked very hard to blend in with these Americans," her voice became soft and appealing again.

"Mr. Markrava, I would very much like you to meet my family. It isn't often we find someone from the old country. We have found the people; from there have more of a…flavor…to their bloodlines." She placed one cool finger to his warm lips to silence him as he started to protest at the lateness of the hour. "We usually dine very late. I am quite sure my family would love to have you for dinner tonight."

Early the next morning

A BURLY SHERIFF red-faced even in the morning's cool air mopped his brow with a linen white handkerchief. He watched the photographer snap one more picture of the still form. The sheriff averted his eyes from the scene before him. Glancing at the half-eaten donut in his hand, he grimaced and tossed it away.

The photographer was suddenly at his side slapping him on the back. "What's a-matter Wayne, not enough cherry filling in that one?" he snickered at his own little joke.

The sheriff glared at him. "You finished, Gary?"

Gary shuffled his feet. "Ya, I got all that I need. Too bad, whoever that was can't say the same. Think Doc Graham will be able to figure out *what* that was, let alone *who*, it was?"

The sheriff only shrugged as he walked back to his car. You'd think after the first one he'd gotten used to seeing things like this. But he doubted he ever would.

MILITARY

Navy Seal

THE DOOR OPENED and she stepped into the bar. Wide-eyed like a deer caught in headlights she stood in the smoky half-light as the door closed soundlessly behind her. Many heads turned her way, many voices stopped mid-sentence. Her long white-blonde tresses cascaded down her back, and it appeared that Alice, or perhaps more appropriately, Red Riding Hood had stepped not into the wolf's lair… but into a lion's den.

Jason Cutter watched as she stood there in the room. She was a breath of fresh air in the stagnant room. His gaze raked her over as did he noticed many others. They noted the expensive jeans and blouse. He also noticed he wasn't the only one to find his body reacting to just how well those clothes hugged her body showing off her figure.

She didn't belong in a place like this, had probably never been to a place like this, so why was she here now?

He saw one of the local troublemakers head her way. Damn. He'd somehow known earlier, this evening just wasn't to come off as planned. He should let her fend for herself, let her find out bars like this weren't for little girls like her. Damn, damn, damn, Jason muttered to himself as he strode over to intercept the local. Why did he always have to play the hero?

Sarah fought not to gag as the smell of beer, cigarettes, and acrid body odor rolled off the large man that slid up in front of her. Dark curly hair escaped from a soiled and stained torn tee shirt. A denim jacket, minus the sleeves, decorated with colorful patches did nothing to conceal arms displaying exotic designed tattoos.

"Hello." She bit back the bile that rose in her throat from his stench.

"Hello, purdy, lady." The man slurred out.

"My those are colorful drawings you have, sir."

"You think so… you should see the one I've got tattooed here." The man had reached for his pants zipper and was beginning to lower it.

A well-muscled man came up to slap the man

in front of her on the back good-naturedly; he was accompanied by two others.

"I think this gentleman needs some assistance, don't you men."

"Yes, sir!"

"Why don't you see he receives the help he needs?"

"Yes, sir, we'll do just that sir." And with that the two grabbed the man with the tattoos under the arms and lead him away.

Jason now faced the woman. "Ma'am, this really isn't a place for a lady to be."

"Yes, it isn't." And with those words she grabbed his hand and tugging on it led him out the door.

"Aha, Ma'am, I'm not sure what you think you're doing..." What the hell had he just gotten himself into.

"It just went thunk and then made a whapping noise, something is wrong with it, and it won't move. Do you think it could be dead?"

"Ma'am... I'm not a vet..." What was dead, an animal and if so what kind of critter was it?

"Well of course you're not, you're not that old."

What in the world did his age have to do with anything he searched his brain for an answer.

"Here it is. Can it be revived you think?"

Jason found himself staring at a car, a car with a flat tire. He closed his eyes for a moment and took a deep breath letting it out very slowly. "Do you have a jack and a spare?" He asked carefully.

"Well, the pack might have a jack in it, but it's been a long time since I used them and a spare what?"

"Huh…" was all Cutter could muster up for a split moment, then. "A car jack, what is used to lift the car so that a spare tire can be put on."

She just looked at him with those big eyes.

"They would be in your trunk."

"Ok." And she handed him the keys to the car.

Several minutes later, she kissed then patted his cheek, slid into the car and drove away smiling while leaving Cutter standing by the side of the road. Jason's luck was in working order as his men, wondering where their Lieutenant had gone, found him. Cutter's growl as he hopped into the jeep stopped all from asking what had happened to the blonde.

The next morning started without any incidents, but that was about to change, and so was his life.

They hadn't exchanged phone numbers or

addresses. Hell, they hadn't even swapped names. Yet here she was. The sun shone brightly, and a soft breeze drifted around him and his men. Lt. Jason Cutter stood there in awe as he watched her slide gracefully from the MP's jeep wondering how she had found him.

How he wondered how she had talked her way onto the base, and into being brought to him. He'd thought she was pretty in the headlights of her car last night but now he realized she was even more beautiful in the daylight. She stopped right in front of him, and he caught the scent of honeysuckle, and sighed before he realized what he'd done.

"Here," she said smiling sweetly handing him a parcel the size of a hatbox. "This is for you." Dubiously he eyed the package wrapped in silver foil adorned with one dark blue and one dark purple ribbon as he took it from her. "It's my way of saying thank you for helping me and possible saving my life last night."

"Thank you, Ma'am, but you…"

"Oh, but I did." She toyed with the bow. "I made one of them blue."

"Blue?"

"Yes." She toyed more with the bow then suddenly looked up straight into his eyes capturing and holding them with her gaze. "Blue was alright, isn't it? It's a Navy color, isn't it?"

"Blue?" He frowned slightly then glanced down at the box then back to her face.

"Navy? Yes, blue is one of the Navy's colors."

"Oh, that's good." She took a deep breath and smiled again. "I wasn't sure which kind you might like so there's six different types in there."

He found himself smiling because she was. "Six different types?" He was having trouble concentrating on the subject at hand, since he couldn't keep himself from being pulled into the depths of her dark sapphire eyes.

She smiled and he found himself swallowing hard. "Yes, six different types. There are chocolate chip, peanut butter, peanut butter chocolate chip, sugar, oatmeal raisin, and frosted butter."

"Frosted butter?"

"Yes, frosted butter. Cookies, Mr. Seal, cookies. In the box." She glanced down at the box.

"Oh, yes." He looked at the box as if seeing it for the first time then back to her.

A team of BUDS ran by rather closely and she tried to step back out of their way. Unfortunately, she stepped back directly into the path of an oncoming jeep. Cutter, still holding the box, grabbed her around the waist, pulling her hard against him and away from the jeep. It was her turn to swallow hard as she looked up into his eyes, "That's twice now."

"Yes Ma'am, that's twice. I guess you'll have to thank me again."

"How?"

"I guess you'll have to marry me." Cutter couldn't believe he'd just said those words, but in that same instant he was happy that he had.

"But you haven't even tasted my cookies." She whispered.

Slowly, he bent his head and brushed his lips over hers before capturing them and deepening the kiss.

The hoots and catcalls first drew Major Carfeld's attention. Next, he saw the small crowd that was steadily growing. He didn't know who was causing this blockade on his grounds, but he was going to see someone's head roll. Carfeld pushed his way through the group and was stunned to find his best instructor smack dab in the middle of the cluster. He came up to Cutter ready to bust him for his lack of military decorum.

"What's the meaning of this sailor?" He barked in his best commanding voice.

"I had to taste this lady's cookies before she would give me an answer, sir."

"An answer, L. T.?"

"Yes, sir an answer." He never took his eyes off her. "Ma'am?"

"Well, if you really like my cookies…"

"Yes, Ma'am. I do."

"Well then, yes. I'll marry you. By the way Mr. Seal, it might be good if you told me your name?"

They'd been married not quite a month. Cutter stood with Sarah beside him as they watched his students practice. He realized he liked having his wife close whenever the decorum permitted.

He glanced over to see her pick up one of the small, throwing knives.

"Honey, becare…" He didn't finish his warning as he watched her flip the small blade from one hand expertly to the next then threw it at the target—hitting it dead center.

"Wow!" said the private who was supposed to be the one practicing. "Was that just a fluke or did you do that on purpose?"

Cutter just shook his head. "Sarah, where did you learn to do that?"

"Barnum and Bailey," she replied as she picked up another knife and repeated her previous throw.

Cutter wore a confused lopsided grin. "The

circus people?"

"Yep. When I did a story about the big top and knife throwers I went to them for advice. Later, when I was good enough, they put me in the show. I used a whip in another."

Cutter came up to her plucking the knife away from her still just a bit unnerved by her handling the razor-sharp instruments. "I don't suppose you used the whip when you worked as a lion tamer."

"No, silly. I am allergic to cats, remember." Sarah laughed at him.

Cutter sighed, "That's good."

She raised an eyebrow. "That I'm allergic to cats?"

He squeezed shut his eyes as he wrinkled his brow. "No, that you weren't a lion tamer."

Sarah hugged him. "I just used the whip when I stripped the clothes off a man while I was riding bare back."

Cutter had been nuzzling Sarah's ear as she spoke and his head jerked up as he realized what she'd said. "Bare back…?"

"The horse was bare back not me, really Jason you should pay more attention to me when I am talking." She shook her head at him frowning. Jason Cutter pulled her tighter to him as he looked skyward for divine help. "I'll try honey, I really will try."

The private walked away quietly mumbling. "She could have been my dream date."

HE IS HOME

HE RETURNS FROM the war to the same old homestead. Nothing has changed. Momma still does her washing by hand; scrubbing, wringing, hanging it out on a line. Little brother does the chores now he used to do… the milking, feeding the cows, helping Poppa with the team and the plowing.

He sees Sarah out feeding the chickens. A chuckle slips out as she fends off the old red rooster. He thinks, "She handled that old bird just as Momma would."

Slowly, ever so slowly, he makes for the house. What tales he'll be able to tell at supper tonight. The sights and sounds of the big cities, here… and over there. He'll tell Momma about machines that do the washing all by themselves. He'll tell of store-bought milk and processed meats. White eggs—not brown—line the shelves.

Poppa will be pleased with the ready-made cigarettes. Knowing Poppa, they'll be saved for special occasions.

In the kitchen, Momma is first to see him. Her firstborn! She sent him into the world a green man-child …and a man came back; always, in her heart, still a small child. Her hands ache. She looks down, sees she has been gripping the dishpan's edges ever so tightly.

Straightening, she tucks a loose strand of hair back in place. With the back of her hand, she wipes tears from her face.

On the front porch and down its steps, she pauses on the last. He sees her and, like her, he pauses, too. He tries to stand a little taller.

"Momma," he whispers. He knows she won't ask, only waiting 'til he can tell. Both smile bravely.

Up the steps, into the house, a mother and son. She, in faded calico. He, in military blue. Pants pressed smartly, one pant leg neatly folded and pinned.

He is home.

DRAGONS

Perhaps Tonight

SHE SAGGED WITH a weary sadness against the bridge's graying wooden railing. Shoulders hunched, her arms hugging her waist, the blowing wind twisted, tangled her rain-soaked hair. Saturated by the elements, her dress clung to her like a second, more colorful, skin. At first, I thought she raised her hand to brush the rain from her face, then realized she wiped at salty tears.

Who was this woman? What brought her to this desolated stretch of road on a night such as this? A night with no moon, a night where black clouds ran from the wind across an even blacker sky.

When had she given up? The spark inside her—was it suddenly snuffed out or fed less and less until it slowly, painfully died away? Why had it been permitted to die at all?

Tightly now, she grips the railing as though it were her last link to what is real and solid in this world.

I wanted to go to her, warm her within my embrace, but I was afraid. Afraid that my presence would frighten her; that if she turned to see me, I would see in her eyes that which frightens me. I know what loneliness is, I know the pain and hunger it brings to a soul—it has been a constant companion of mine for far too long.

I could give so much to this woman. If she were to accept me as I am, we could be so very happy together. Never would she want for anything. Rare metals and precious gems would be hers only for the asking. The finest oriental silks would cover her bed, and only exotic fabrics and perfumes would caress her body.

I could take her to far away, exciting mystic places for adventures. Knowledge, I could share with her the knowledge of the ages. If only....

I would gladly do all of this and more. I would willingly give this woman my heart, my soul, my love if I truly believed it would erase her loneliness...and mine.

I hear someone approaching. I slip back into the shadows unseen. It is a man. He sees her, relief shows on his face. He pauses; she turns as if in a dream. He reaches out with outstretched arms. His eyes are pleading. Though his own pain he tells her, asks her, "I am sorry. Please forgive me."

She bites her lower lip and hesitates, waiting, wanting more from him. He chokes back a sob before he says the words, "I love you."

It is there. Dimly, weakly, it flickers, but it is there, again, in her eyes, that tiny spark.

She goes to him, tightly they hold each other. I close my eyes, imagining how it would feel to be in such an embrace, to feel another's body close to mine.

The man takes off his coat, places it gently on her shoulders. His arm goes around her to comfort and support her. Now they are leaving, soft whispered tones drift back to me on the wind.

Alone, in the night I stand. I feel a tear mix with the rain as it slides down my cheek now. A shiver runs along my spine. I shake the rain from my wings, my scales jingle an ancient music, long forgotten. I feel the wind in my face, my wings stretch, catching it, I rise.

Maybe I am the last. My hope that I am not keeps me searching. Perhaps tonight, somewhere else, another dragon flies the sky.

Newspaper Photograph

It all began with the local paper arriving one night. Something so simple in most people's lives, something so very devastating in mine. Upon seeing the picture for the first time my reaction was one of disbelief, but then I looked at it again. It was him, smiling, shaking hands, handsome as I always knew he would be, ironic that last thought about him being handsome. The first time we met I trembled with fear at the sight of him… yet longed to run my hands over him. Shaking my head as though this would clear the muzzyness from it I reached for the telephone to call the local paper.

The woman at the paper was polite but other than the few details they had they knew nothing more about the man in the picture. He was a wealthy entrepreneur who had come to our small town to launch a major business. He was single (the woman assumed this but he neither denied nor confirmed this when questioned). His personal life was just that personal, maybe that was because no one could find out anything about his personal life. His and his family's business ventures were well documented, maybe too well documented. I asked her if it was possible to obtain the information the paper had, she replied it was.

Hurrying, I dressed and went to town all of this achieved with trembling hands and numb fingers. It couldn't be him, yet it was. So different and so much the same. Sitting now in my car with the information I read and re-read the one single page. This was not happening, it couldn't be him, why not a small inner voice asked. Because I shot back you know what it means if it is him.

Trapped, a cold sweat washed over me I lay my head on the steering wheel, so tired of it all. The never knowing of what was… and what wasn't any more. It glared at me from an offset line on the copy. Yes, this would be the only way to find out if it was really him or not… and a way for me to find out if….

He was to be at the groundbreaking ceremony today at one this afternoon, and the public was welcome. Asking directions, I soon found the site of the business that was to breathe life into our dying community. It wasn't long before others started showing up, car after car, which one was his? A long black limo pulled up, our mayor and several other town leaders exited it. Funny I don't remember holding my breath the entire time, not until I saw the top of his head and released my breath did I realize it. He and the others were walking to a semi enclosed roped off area. I was too far away to be sure if it really was him. I had to get closer. Pushing and shoving, people were packed together like Japanese in a Tokyo subway. The air was thick, hot and weighed down on me heavily as I struggled through the crowd. Yes, I was almost there I could clearly hear the men's voices. Soon… soon I would know. What… what… was happening? The crowd was breaking up the ceremony was over, they were leaving… HE… was leaving!

As if in a dream… hysterical laughter bubbled in me… of course this had to… but it was not. I shoved and pushed passed people to reach that small group of men. Someone, a guard? Grabbed at my arm, jerking free from him I stumbled, regained my footing, fifteen feet, ten feet I was almost there. Two guards grabbed me by the arms. A cry of "NO!" tore from my lips. My struggles against my immovable captors were useless, but my cry had reached… HIS… ears.

He stopped and slowly he turned towards me. It… was… HIM! How could this be? He began to walk to where the guards held me or was it my own disbelief that held me. Closer he came, now he signaled the guards to release me. Flashing a bright smile, a smile I knew. Eyes that danced sparkled with amusement, eyes that I knew. He came up to me reaching out a hand to caress my cheek, a *man's* hand, so different than before. "Hello Genevieve." His voice rich and vibrating a voice I thought I once heard in a dream.

A voice I heard late one night. A voice now in… another form.

I closed my eyes savoring his touch, rejoicing in the knowledge that it was truly him. Taking the hand that caressed my face in my hand, I kissed his palm gazing into his eyes. Smiling through tears of relief and joy I replied.

"Hello my Dragon."

GHOSTS

Intruders

"VERN, VERN, WAKE up."

"Huh, what?"

"I heard a noise."

"It's probably the wind, Shelly."

"No, it wasn't the wind. I heard, there, there did you hear that? I bet it's those kids again."

"I'll go look; you stay here."

"I will not."

"Ok, just stay behind me, ok?"

"Ok."

Vern swung his feet off the bed looking for his slippers, then remembered, sighed, grabbed his robe and pulled it on. He headed out the bedroom door to the top of the steps, Shelly right behind him. Slowly Vern went down one step then the next.

"Vern?"

"Shush, Shell."

"I think they're in the living room, bet they're here to steal the TV."

"I don't think they want our TV, Shell."

"It's a Technicolor Magnavox why wouldn't they want it?"

"Because," Vern sighed. "Never mind, please be quiet."

Down two more steps, and Vern went to the next, it moaned loudly in protest. Vern and Shelly froze. Shelly's hand shot out grabbing Vern's arm, he winched as her nails dug in.

"Shell?"

"What Vern?"

"Ease up on my arm, ok?"

"Oh, sorry dear." She patted his arm smoothing down the material bunched there.

"It's ok, honey," sighed Vern.

Down two more steps, then two more.

The sound of footsteps coming down the hallway from the kitchen towards them.

Vern heard Shelly's sharp intake of breath at his ear.

Shuffling.

Muffled voices.

Something, glass? Crashed to the floor Vern and Shelly jumped where they were.

"Vern?"

"It's ok, honey you're safe with me."

Footsteps, coming closer, closer, closer.

Vern and Shelly hovered on the last step.

"Aaaaaaaaaaaahhhhhhhhhhhaaaaaaa!"

"RUN!"

"GET OUTTA MY WAY!"

"YOU, GET OTTA MY WAY!"

"THE DOOR, HEAD FOR THE FRONT DOOR!"

The heavy oak door swung open with a bang hard enough to rattle the lead glass inserts. A gust of chilled October wind slammed the screen door flat on the house siding. They ran head long into the blue and red strobe lights bathing the outside of the house waiting for them.

Vern patted his wife's back. "Shell, Shell, it's ok, I've got you. See the police have showed up everything is going to be alright." Vern held his trembling wife to him her face buried in the crook of his shoulder. Gently, he brushed back a lock of her hair from her face and placed a kiss to her quivering lips.

Shelly sobbed. "Why, why do they haunt us, Vern? Every year it's the same thing."

"They're just kids, they're young and foolish, but the police are here, they'll take them away."

He hugged her close, and she leaned on him until her shaking stopped.

Halfway up the stairs Shelly pause, "I love you, Vern."

"I love you, Shell." Vern wrapped an arm around Shelly's shoulders, and together they softly floated back up the stairs.

Moonville Tunnel

KEVIN STOOD AT the Moonville Tunnel mouth, hands on his hips, surveying the area. Dead dry vines hung like gnarled mummified fingers over the entrance. The passageway length was dark, and dank. A breeze wafting from the opening was cemetery musty causing him to wrinkle his nose in disgust.

Raising his left arm, he checked his watch. His friends Jim and Alan were over an hour late. Kevin chuckled, they most likely chickened out of the dare. Two nights back they made a pack to be here today at noon to travel the tunnel and explore the giant cuckoo clock on the other side. Well, if they weren't going to show he still wanted to see the once popular attraction.

He stepped from the bright sunlight into the darkness switching on a penlight to help guide his way. Who knew what called this corridor home no use stepping on some critter and ticking it off. As Kevin got closer to the end, he marveled at the brightly painted structure, the still working clock and the animated animals and people that shuffled back and forth. Funny the guys had told him the clock was in disrepair but here it was ticking away merrily. The paint appeared fresh and vivid, the works whirled and clicked clear and sharp.

Kevin took his time circling the building and well-kept grounds. Lush green grass encircled the area while vibrant multicolored tulips danced in the gentle breeze. Coming back to the front façade, he heard the gears switching to announce the hour. The music gathered note by note rising and ebbing in a light melody. That's when he noticed the sky beginning to tumble dark with menacing clouds. Before his eyes the paint faded and pealed as the smiling faces of the character's grew frowns and…were those teeth?

The wind picked up blowing dried brush and rubbish around into a mini swirl. One piece of paper tore from a nearby pole to smack him in the face. Kevin swiped it from him only to stare in disbelief at the flyer's print. Faded and rain stained the paper announced the closing of the clock and the date of its demolition. No, oh no, this couldn't be true, the date was from fifty years ago.

Kevin stumbled back as the storybook creature's step by step began to descend on him. He screamed, picked up a rock, flinging it at one. It bounced off the wooden automaton with a dull thud. Staggering back, he struggled to make his body and mind work in tandem. Finally finding purchase he sprinted down the tunnel. His shrieks of terror reverberated off the stone walls. He was nearly at the other entrance. He could see the light. Hands reached from the darkness tearing at his clothes. His feet pounded the dirt jarring his legs and thighs. The end, the end was three steps away when darkness churned around him, dragging him to the ground.

"Kevin, Kevin it's you it's really you." A voice strangled by age wheezed.

"I can't believe it's really you." The other man choked out. "We thought you'd disappeared or worse was dead."

Kevin sat on the ground and raised a hand to block out the bright sun to see who stood over him. Two old men gnarled and bent by age. One leaned on a cane gazed down on him.

"Boy, what happened to you? You don't look

a day over twenty-five how is that possible?"

"Jim? Alan? Is it really you? Why do you look so old? What happened? Why didn't you come out today?"

Between the older men they helped him to his feet.

"Today? Son, we came out that day nearly fifty years ago looking for you."

"Never found you, we figured you stood us up, so we went home."

"But I did show up and I went to the clock and, and I'm not sure what occurred after that."

"Kevin, we came back the next day and several after that no one knew where you were. We found your car but not you."

"For the past fifty years we came out here on the anniversary of your disappearance hoping to find, well something of you."

"And here you are."

Kevin spun squinting his eyes to peer down the tunnel, but there was no opening, only a collapsed rubble of a bygone era.

"I remember. I went through the tunnel. I saw the clock. I heard it chime. The characters, the characters, they chased me."

The wind blustered and rain began to spat upon them.

"We got your car here well take you home, okay?"

They patted him on the back and shuffled to the car, once inside they trio traveled down the dusty forgotten road, again. The same as they did every year.

HUMOR

The Virus

"Ow," I MUTTERED as the nurse jabbed the needle into to my shoulder.

"Sorry," the nurse replied as she then smiled a bit too cheerily kind of like the Joker in the Batman movies. She applied a Band-Aid to the injured spot. "You're all safe now from the COVID virus."

"Sure, whatever." I muttered.

As soon as this virus popped up my kids and many others around town got the idea that the elderly like myself would be safer in the prestigious gated Dr. Moreau Community. Oh, sure I questioned their logic and the fact this place always had openings. The kids wouldn't listen to my concerns about the residence never being crowded. I guess they thought the rumors of me having tons of royalty money from my books was real. I'd love to see their faces when they went through my important papers and found nothing green in the boxes downstairs except the mold from the damp basement.

Dr. Moreau's Community Housing for the elderly was nice in the beginning. Our rooms were pleasant, decorated in a jungle theme, bright colors and all. The meals were gourmet five star delicious, and I met several wonderful people. There was Stan, a banker, Marla, a model for Vogue in her day who still retained her great looks, Mary Beth, a housewife, grandmother, and baker of blue-ribbon pies. George, a used cars salesman who'd had a very lucrative business in town, Chuck, a several times elected mayor in town and me. In the beginning we ate together, lounged around the heated pool and late night poker games. Sometimes regular Texas Hold'em sometimes strip. It all depended on who's social security check got cashed first and who got to smuggle in the Viagra.

The six of us stuck together and commented in private hushed tones about the population of the community. It fluctuated from big to small each week. At first, we were fine, then Marla didn't show up one day. The staff said she'd passed in her sleep of natural causes. The next was

George, heart attack in the steam room. Strange because George didn't like humidity. Mary Beth after that with no real cause of death explained. Then Stan and Chuck got hit by lightning on the golf course on a clear and sunny day.

Now it was down to just me.

So here I was in the "community's" health office receiving yet another injection for this new virus. The government's sudden announcement of this health crisis with its constant changing rules on how to handle it had me and others questioning the daily health updates. Wear gloves, don't wear gloves. Wear a mask, don't wear a mask. Shelter in place, except when it's time to get the next round of inoculations then let's board a party bus to the clinic!

The elderly were asking too many questions according to the younger generation, we needed to let the government take care of us. We elderly replied, the government can't take care of itself; how do we expect it to take care of us? Our children patted us on the head and did their best to sooth us with nonsense platitudes. We weren't buying the bull droppings on the floor, but we wanted our children to be right, so we agreed to their 'precautions'.

So here I sat in a sterile white, windowless room.

I stood and promptly sat back down as my stomach rolled and heaved like a ship in a bad storm. "Excuse me nurse, I'm not feeling well."

"Oh, honey it's okay, some of our patients have that after their last shot." She called for another attendant who appeared way too quickly with a wheelchair. They helped me into the device and rolled me down a long hallway to finally a double door with 'exit' splashed in red. My vision blurred and I felt my body slump to one side as everything went black.

The smell of salt air filled my nose and coated the inside of my mouth. Speaking of my mouth it felt bigger, longer, and when I went to extend my tongue to lick my lips, I slapped the side of my face! Startled, I jerked my head back and caught sight of something reflected off a metal cabinet. I peered closer and tilted my head and so did the reflection in front of me. Bringing my hand up to touch my face so did the creature in front of me. That's when I noticed my hand. The powerful muscled and deadly clawed appendage of a Kimono Dragon was where my arm and hand should be.

I shook my head and so did the Dragon.

Something fluttered behind my head and down my neck.

Cautiously I profiled my head and so did the Dragon, long crimson red hair like an Oar Fish's flowed down my head, across my back to my tail.

TAIL!?

What the heck!

I turned so fast my new tail smacked the cage holding me with enough force to bend the bars. Flicking my tail again I made the opening bigger, one more time and the bars shredded like tissue paper.

I was free!

The door to the room burst open with several people rushing in guns aimed and snag ropes ready.

"Grrrrrrrrrr, hiss!" A tremendous growl rose from my throat exploding from me with a vicious snap of a mouthful of needle-sharp teeth followed.

The humans danced back screaming. I rushed for the exit, one human tried to stop me, and I ran straight over him. Another outside with a snare rope confronted me and I spun and swiped his legs out from under him with my thick glorious tail.

I scurried off down a jungle trail; a familiar scent caught my attention and off I went. The sweet musky smell led me to a large body of water. Hearing the humans closing fast I plunged into the salty water. I swam for hours, my now powerful limbs taking me far into deep blue waters. The scent from earlier in my snout spurned me onward. The bright sun began to dip into the inky night. Finally, when I thought I couldn't swim any more sand met my feet and I climbed onto a beach and slept.

"Grrrrr?" a soft rumble woke me. Another like me had an orange-red fruit in its mouth which it dropped then nudged to me.

I gobbled down the delight; it quenched my thirst and nourished me at the same time.

The other ran off but just as quickly came back with another fruit which he offered again.

He was a big fellow, with massive muscles and a handsome dew lap of orange, blue, and bright green. I liked that dew lap a lot. There was something familiar about his eyes.

He came closer, his snout touched mine and his scent filled me. The aroma that brought me here.

Now on my feet again I returned the greeting with a snout bump of my own.

His eyes lit up and I suddenly knew who he was!

"STAN!" I wanted to cry out, but only a grrrrr, hiss, gulp, escaped my mouth.

He lifted his head, gave three head jerks and responded with his own grrrrr, hiss, gulp.

It 'was' Stan!

I rubbed my head along his neck so happy to see him.

Stan maneuvered his massive size back and with more head bobbing encouraged me to follow him. We scurried along the beach to a jungle trail passing more and more creatures like us. Until we came to the beginning of a stone outcropping. I could hear human voices and hung back afraid. Stan cuddled up to me flicking his tongue along my neck then backing off wanting me to trust him. Guardedly I shadowed him. High on a rock ledge lay George and Marla, their manes of scarlet fluttered in the soft breeze. A blue and white tender boat bobbing on the water held a dozen or more passengers with cameras. The clicking, whirring, and shouts of the people drifted to us.

"Where did they come from?"

"There's so many of them?"

"Aren't they beautiful?"

"I've never seen this species before!"

"Upload these pictures to the internet! This is the biggest news story ever!"

Best Friend

THE MUG WARMED my hands but not completely thawing the cold from them. Only Maxwell holding them with his could chase the chill away and that was never going to happen again. Sunlight filtered through the curtains drawing me to the window. Dust motes rode the bright beams of light like a sparkling bridge into the room.

The dogwood we planted sported buds this morning green, now soon to turn into soft pink and white petals.

"You knew it would come to an end." Pepe whispered from his seat on the sofa.

"I know, I just didn't…" and couldn't finish.

"Oh, come now, you *did* know." Pepe insisted.

"Oh, no I didn't truly." I choked it out.

"You did, stop with this nonsense." He stomped his foot. "You knew and ignored the signs, and they were there bright and flashing."

"Yes, you're right you're always right."

"Of course, I am, I'm French we can always tell things of love. Their beginning and end."

"But why now?"

"Why did I put an end to it?"

"Yes."

"Because you deserve better and it was easier for me to do it than you."

I sat on the sofa and Pepe laid his head in my lap. "Thank you."

"Always for you." Pepe rose whipping the tear on my cheek away with his tongue.

"You told the police the truth, Maxwell tripped over your French Bull dog and fall down the stairs. He broke his neck."

"Yes, Pepe I didn't lie you're such a good dog, perhaps we should go to the park today."

"Yes, that would be nice."

Marvelous Menagerie

Jeweler and Gem

Doré works in an architectural office as part of a middle management secretarial staff.

A small part.

She fills in whenever and wherever someone needs clerical help. In other words, she holds a position one step above a glorified gofer. She usually works in the back corner cubicle. Everyone knows the area, the area where no one goes without first acquiring their immunization shots and a map. Then one day someone forgot to update their vaccination records, and the flu took out three-fourths of the building employees. Doré found herself working for the CEO.

Lucky?

Many find that there is a fine, faint line between having luck or being cursed.

Doré was embarrassed to realize the staff were the first to notice, then Fred, her boss, picked up on the fact his best customer was dropping by nearly daily to talk to her. Well, Fred has been known to use any tactic to keep patrons coming back. Fred started hinting (a sledgehammer has more tact than Fred) Doré should be nicer to Mr. Skavendale. She informed him her job entailed only secretarial work from nine to five and nothing, under any circumstances, else. Fred being Fred just winked at her saying, "Sure whatever you say," and winked at her again before swaggering into his office. Fred was literally jumping for joy when Mr. Skavendale started making excuses to stop by more and more. Not that Mr. Skavendale wasn't an important, valuable client to begin with, but he could have had any number of people checking on the work the firm was doing for him. He didn't have to involve himself, and lately he wasn't talking to the supervisors. He spoke with Doré, and not only about business.

Oh, how Doré wished her job didn't pay so well, have great hours, or incredible benefits, but sadly she needed it all. At forty, having a double-digit number of one-night dates behind her, being unmarried, and without any future prospects, well, one needs to look after one's self.

Cinderella was a fairy tale and nothing else.

Doré knew what Dimitri, he'd asked her to call him by his first name, was leading up to. It had happened enough and she should have stopped him before he acted. Yet, she hoped for and dreaded for the possibility of the event in the same heartbeat.

"Why must Mr. Skavendale be so incredibly handsome, sexy or polite?" She thought to herself. *"He isn't the type of man you can brush off with a knitted brow and hooded glance or if need be, a sharp word. Besides, Mr. Skavendale had never been discourteous or overstepped his bounds in his visits with me. He'd always been a gentleman. "Doré," he calls me with his accent, filled voice. "Doré the golden one—a maiden, fair, topaz-crowned, with azure eyes he recites to me."*

On the afternoon of the big day, she ate her brown-bag lunch alone in a quiet part of the building's courtyard, but she could hear the other workers whispering and talking about the possible events tonight might bring. The night's possibilities and why would a man such as he asks someone like her out on a date?

"Oh, why did I say yes?" Doré asked herself.

A gown of blue silk with matching shawl,

shoes, and purse had been waiting along with a messenger on her door step the day before. Nestled inside the fabric's rich folds was a note saying if the size was wrong or the color she could return it, but he hoped he'd guessed right about both. Doré sighed. He had, of course.

Dimitri Skavendale knew he was out of his league with this woman. She hadn't the faintest idea of how beautiful she really was or how utterly right she was for him. He would have to pull out all the stops to convince her of what he already knew.

They were made for each other.

"Well, here they were." They each thought.

Doré fought not to fidget as she glanced around *"He brought me here tonight to this place, to this, in his words, 'suitable eating establishment.' He, with his refined and sophisticated ways. Why did I let him talk me into coming here?* She flipped her hair back over her shoulder, willing it to stay where she'd put it and adjusted her glasses, again. She felt as if everyone was staring at her. She even told him this.

Dimitri laughed, smiled and whispered in her ear, "Of course they're staring, people usually notice beautiful things." He was certainly noticing her, and the envious looks' others were sending their way.

She raised one eyebrow. *"Is that what I am? A beautiful thing?"* She snorted unlady-like as that thought crossed her mind. *"He and they must have seen someone or something else. Not me, but... What fascinates him about me? What first drew him... to me? I am me. Ordinary and boring. I don't belong here, not in this place slathered in its elegance. He, on the other hand."*

"I wonder why she agreed to this dinner date. Is she going to wait until the evening is over to tell me to take a flying leap or will she cut me to shreds before the entree is even served? She is so incredibly beautiful." He waved the waiter away and held out her chair for her.

They dined on food and wine he'd carefully selected. Hors d'oeuvres of caviar pie and shrimp he hoped would delight her and with chocolate dipped strawberries and apricots he tempted her. Champagne and a fine Bordeaux followed. The first entree was Wine Broth served in a brandy snifter. Wine Broth is a delicate mixture of chicken and pork broth blended with a clear red wine. Served warm, is a delightful experience for one's mouth he told her as she dubiously eyed her glass. When she tried it, she found it indeed was delicious. Roast corn crab soup and a crisp arugula, water crest and salad green mélange with warm walnut dressing were next.

Seafood crepes stuffed with chunks of lobster, crab and shrimp teased their appetites. Finally, the main course came a generous serving of Beef Wellington with warmed pop-overs, ginger glazed carrots and green bean almandine.

He held his breath as he watched her marvel and cringe at his worldly ways. She was so quiet keeping her mouth shut and her hands folded in her lap between each course served. He smiled and carried the conversation expertly, gazing at her the entire time. His dark laughing eyes watching her every move. Occasionally, Dimitri reached down to hold her hand, brushing his thumb over her knuckles. Feeling the softness of her skin wanting to take her in his arms, he knew it was yet too soon.

"I can't breathe." Doré thought, feeling her chest tightening as he held her hand.

She excused herself. Dimitri stood, suit jacket unbuttoned, hands loosely clasped behind his back, staring at her, knowing he wears that smug smile that only tugs at the corners of his mouth. He senses she is afraid, but he's not sure of what. Him?

Doré's inner-self whispers, *"No longer safe and*

secure with myself am I, for whenever I turn, he is there watching."

Across the room she pauses to look back at him. She watches as a woman glossy like a page from an expensive magazine, tall in heels, slick skirted, frightfully pale-haired, now slides up to him. Doré notes she, this woman, is everything that men usually notice in a woman. Doré grits her teeth. The other woman is a zircon shiny, bright and manmade, or in this case woman made, but not a diamond fresh mined dirty and dark. Nor is she, this woman who is waiting for the skilled hand of the jeweler to find the true gem hiding in its depths. Doré glances over to him, *"Is he to be my jeweler?"* She wonders.

She wants to shout, *"Take him, he is nothing to me! And I… I am nothing to him,"* but her words are only an echoing whisper in her head followed by an annoying laughter from somewhere else deep inside her.

Doré watches as Dimitri politely chats with the woman. He smiles. The woman believes it is at the clever words she has spoken. He and she, shamefully she, realizes her embarrassed, jealous blush has made him smile. He glances down to the woman giving her his attention, secure in the moment Doré won't leave.

Dimitri now knows her secret fear and his smile broadens. Tied is she, by his invisible tether. Does she know, he knows?

"I am not his lap dog, nor will I stay rooted like a dog given one command waiting for the next." She wants to stamp her foot and shout. Instead, she lets him see her defiantly thrust her chin up and turn on her heel. She escapes into the ladies' room with his wide grin and dancing eyes burning into her back.

Dimitri stifles a chuckle, *"She knows, she knows! Oh, if he can only complete the seduction."* He prays as she disappears into the facilities.

Readjust, reapply, rebuild her self-confidence. She looks in the mirror at her reflection to find the outside is polished again, the inside… She takes a deep breath and slowly lets it out… now… she is ready. Recharged, she opens the door, boldly stepping back into the hallway expecting to see as so many other dates… he is gone. *"No, she won't think about it."* She straightens her shoulders.

He is there… alone… unwaveringly waiting for her.

Her confidence soars as she realizes she wanted him to be there. To her he is intelligent, handsome, sexy and strong. She thinks she is plain, average, weak, and terribly insecure.

To him she is the most intelligent, beautiful, sexy and strong woman he's ever met. She isn't concerned about his wealth; in fact, she appears to be embarrassed by it and he is thrilled.

He waits for her… only her.

Her jeweler.

His gem.

CHEAITOO

CHEAITOO STOOD, ARMS raised; his call of unrestrained power echoed back to him through the night air. He was a figure silhouetted by the full moon—half man, half wolf. Moving with fluid ease, he made his way down through the tangled brush and briers, towards the meadow clearing, a dagger clenched between his jaws. He raced to battle the Bruja for the last time. Cheaitoo prayed to his gods not for victory for himself, not for release from his own torment, but for the safety of his people, and his mate.

In the meadow, a flame of azure tall as a grown man burned brightly. As Cheaitoo approached, it began to form grotesquely into the Bruja.

Cheaitoo advanced towards the Bruja, snatching the weapon from his jaws, he swung his arm in a meticulous arc, first one way then the other, wielding the dagger with masterful grace.

The Bruja smiled, a wide, gaping-hole grin. As Cheaitoo approached, it laughed. "Weakling man. You think to challenge me?" it screeched.

"Yes! I would challenge you, witch!" shouted Cheaitoo, circling.

"Then come to me, little man. Come closer so that I may have the pleasure of crushing you," it sneered.

Through the desolate village, a lone camp dog, tail tucked between its scrawny legs, skulked aimlessly. It came to one tent, froze, one forepaw up. Sniffing the air, it uttered a low growl at the figure before it, then fled into the darkness.

The figure knelt in front of the tent that had once lodged the great shaman of the village, her teacher. Her stepfather. Now Permelia raised the stone bowl with one hand as she sprinkled the tansis root into the darkened mixture, swirling it slowly, remembering the words and teachings of her father to his outlander child.

"Barat drew we nis." Gods of my Gods. "Tay hone na nese ha." Hear me and answer my plea. Permelia lifted her face to the night sky. "Give wisdom, and strength, give him courage to defeat the witch, the Bruja. Grant all of this to Cheaitoo, ruler of our people, my lord and mate, sire of that which grows within me." She flung the mixture into the cooking fire's flames before her, igniting the air around her for an instant.

Cheaitoo lunged, slicing with the dagger, only to find himself cutting through air. The Bruja had vanished, only to reappear a few steps away. Cheaitoo knew he must place the odds in his favor or face defeat…and death.

"You have no honor, witch! You give me no honor to fight you!" he shouted.

"No honor?" The Bruja lifted one eyebrow. "I am the greatest of all the gods! How can you say I am without honor?" it growled.

"If you had honor, you would fight me as a man would! Yet you play me like the hunter that hooks a large fish. You fight me like a god. Should I spread my arms wide and await my death like the fish?" He prayed his deception would work.

Permelia closed her eyes, palms open outward, shielding her eyes. The shimmering night air shaped and re-shaped itself before her. One after another, the old gods appeared, forming a circle around her. "Cran nis pa tay ho na cee? Why do you call us, daughter of the night, healer to our people?"

Permelia hid her face, afraid to gaze on the

ancient ones, least she offends them. "I call upon you to lend your power to a brave warrior who fights alone tonight."

"Then raise your eyes, daughter and see us." Permelia beheld the great Silver-tip Grizzly, blinked, then realized it was a shaman's body clothed as a grizzly. The other gods were dressed as the animals her people worshipped. The blood-red Stag of the hot winds, the Turtle, who carried the land on his back, and the great Salmon that could feed an entire village from his body alone. "We know of the warrior Cheaitoo, of whom you speak. He does not fight alone tonight," said the Silvertip.

Permelia scrambled to her feet. "Then you will help him? You will go now to see that the Bruja is defeated for all time?"

"No, daughter." His voice rumbled soft and low, comfortingly. "Cheaitoo does not need our help, when he has the help of so many others."

"Fight you in man form? I find this amuses me. I will fight you as one warrior to one warrior, and I will still defeat you." The Bruja's form clouded and swirled to settle into that of a warrior of ancient times. A warrior who now wielded a deadly otlotl, a club. This otlotl was carved from a tree now a long time gone. Narrow and rippled it started, the better to fill a man's sturdy grip. Thickening even more, it swelled to a bulbous end, its length studded with wicked strips of sharpened stone. Burned black to strengthen it to almost-stone, then painted with the symbols of all the gods.

The ancient warrior moved in quickly, lunging, bringing the otlotl down in a deadly swipe. Cheaitoo dodged to his left, but not before the weapon ripped a bloody gash in his forearm. Swiftly, he darted back and in, to leave a rent across the ancient one's chest. Stunned, the Bruja stepped back, raising a hand to wipe at the bleeding, stinging slash. Howling in rage, it raised its club, charging Cheaitoo. The otlotl clipped the side of Cheaitoo's head, sending him reeling to the ground. The Bruja stood over him, gripping the otlotl in both hands, raising it over his head.

Cheaitoo shook the blackness that threatened to close in on him. Instinctively, his legs shot out, catching the Bruja, knocking him to the ground. Cheaitoo tightened his grip on the dagger and rolled over onto the witch, forcing him on to his back. Grunting with effort, each tried to plunge the dagger into the other. Blood and sweat stung Cheaitoo's eyes, blinding him. Giving a mighty groan, the Bruja flung Cheaitoo onto his back, knocking the breath from him. His opponent slammed a knee into his side. Ribs cracked. He lost his hold on the dagger.

Permelia clutched at her stomach protectively, staring at the gods, confused. "But no others went with him!"

The Silvertip smiled gently. "Oh, but they did. Cheaitoo went tonight armed not only with his dagger, but with the hope, the determination of this village to be free of the Bruja. He went armed with his love for you and your unborn child. So, you see daughter, with an army such as that, he does not fight alone!"

The witch snatched up the fallen weapon; it drew back, intending to plunge the blade deep into the fallen man's chest. It paused, sneering. "You have fought well, little man. Now you will die a warrior's death."

Cheaitoo groped blindly for something…anything…then his hand fell on a hardened, tapered shape. He gripped the otlotl's handle.

One by one, the gods evaporated, leaving only the fire's smoke hanging in the night air. Suddenly, a branch snapped under a heavy foot. Permelia whirled towards the sound.

There Cheaitoo stood—tired, bloodied, his wolf robe torn and hanging. He raised his arms to chant the warrior's victory song, only to have them filled with Permelia. As they stood there, locked in a lovers' embrace, the villagers emerged from their tents, filling the air with voices, each chanting the warrior's victory song.

She Shouldn't Have Been Sacked

No, she shouldn't have been sacked. Day after day she did his bidding, bringing him coffee. Filing and not filing the documents in the right places. Keeping three not two ledgers of company books for him, showing one to the investors, a different set to his wife and the last hidden for all but him. She turned over more soil and dropped it in the hole. She kept telling phone callers and dropper-byes he was busy, couldn't be disturbed. Ha! What he really was doing alone back there in his luxury office with his big screen T.V. hooked up to his computer was surfing the porn sites. She knew because she caught him one day with his pants down and…she shuddered at the memory while shoving the spade sharp and deep into the earth. She shouldn't have been sacked. She turned over a good size clod and dumped onto the squirming mass beside the smaller still one at the bottom of the hole. The squirming mass made an oomph sound when the shovel's contents collided with what she supposed was his stomach. She shouldn't have been sacked. All she'd wanted was one afternoon off, was that too much to ask after nearly thirty years with him? Her cat had died that morning, and she wanted the afternoon off to bury her friend and mourn but nooooo, he'd thrown a hissy fit and called her all sorts of terrible names and then sacked her.

The lamp was right there on his desk. A heavy brass piece with a dark blue shade. The new lamp and shade would be a pretty white and mauve piece, and she must remember to have the office painted on Monday after she cleaned up this weekend. No one would miss him, not even his wife, especially when her allowance would be tripled. Yes, the wall behind his desk would need to be painted. It should be white to match her new office furniture in her new office. She shouldn't have been sacked. She dumped in two more shovel loads of dirt and patted them down. She stood back and admired the re-landscaped area beside the company parking lot. Not a bad day's work with her usual multi-tasking abilities.

She was able to put her troubles and Mr. Fluffy to rest after all.

TOMMY LEE

TOMMY LEE OR a rattler; of the two the snake had the sweeter disposition. Women were drawn to his rugged, six foot-three frame, gravel voice, with his lone wolf gaze and manner. That is, until they realized why lone wolves are…alone. They're dangerous. Not that Tommy Lee would have struck a woman, something only a yellow-belly skunk would do. Naaa, a real man, a man of the same mold as the Duke, would never raise his hand to the weaker sex. Nope. Tommy Lee knew just how to deal with the fillies. You put them in their place and that was on their backs or on their knees. Tommy Lee hated kids like some people hated small, yappy dogs. A boot in the rump was what they could usually expect from him. And that's how Tommy Lee came to be at the ass end of pushing horns.

He didn't mind the job, someone had to do it, it might as well be him. He didn't even mind the dust that covered him and everything else around like flies on a manure pile. What he did mind, was the foreman docking him a days pay for the whole thing. The little varmint had had it coming. Following him all around the ranch asking more questions than a body could stand! The little coyote (and he'd yelped like one of the critters when Tommy Lee had planted his boot) just plain had it coming. Anyway, how was he supposed to know the pup was the whelp of the new boss.

The new boss! Never, in all his born days had he had a…a…*woman*…for a boss! And she just didn't have one whelp…she had a whole damn litter. Yup, a damn litter is what she had, 'cause anything as many as six counted as a litter. He knew that for a fact!

If he'd known that old man Simms had left the ranch to his niece and not a man, like he ought to have done—well, Tommy Lee thought, he'd never have signed on for another year. Another whole year! Damn! It was too late to try and sign on with any of the other ranches, at least any of the better ranches. Damn, a woman boss! It just wasn't natural!

The other hands didn't seem to mind working for a woman, but then they were a bunch of squat pissers any way.

He was interrupted in his thoughts as a steer veered off from the herd. The three of them—Tommy Lee, his pony and the steer—plunged into the scrub brush. The dang stupid beast dodged this way and that way, forcing Tommy Lee to lay flat against his pony to keep from being knocked off.

Then it happened! In all his 36 years it had only happened to him once before and then he'd been a whelp himself. The steer jumped and dodged one way, his pony went another way…and Tommy Lee went sailing another.

To the eye, the prickly-pear cactus with its purple or white flowers is a thing of beauty. Luck had been with Tommy Lee when he landed. He'd not even come close to the cacti. Yup, as he stood up dusting off, glancing back at the cacti spread behind him, he thought he'd been damn lucky. He froze at the sound of the first snort, then turned slowly as a hoof scraped the ground. Old man, Simms out of respect for the breed, had kept a longhorn bull on the ranch. A rangy, old, evil-tempered example of the breed. Even for a breed known for their caginess and unpredictable nature, Old Loco—as he was called—made the rest of the breed seem almost tame, even docile. Old Loco was every cowhand's worst nightmare.

Tommy Lee shifted his gaze from the bull to the cacti, took a deep breath and let out a war whoop that would have made any Indian proud. Unfortunately, he was General Custer, Old Loco was Sitting Bull and this was Little Big Horn. Old Loco went straight for Tommy Lee; Tommy Lee, after a moment's prayer dove into the cacti.

His luck was changing…and not for the better. Rattlesnakes like cool protected areas to sleep during the day. Areas such as under rock ledges, old decaying logs…or prickly-pear cacti patches.

Tommy Lee was retreating into the cacti as fast as he could muttering loudly since the cacti was welcoming him with open spiny arms. Old Loco, even though being a dumb old bull knew better than to follow Tommy Lee into the cacti. Matter of fact as far as Old Loco was concerned, he'd done what he'd set out to do: scare the intruder away from what he considered his private grazing place. Tommy Lee was too preoccupied in his retreat he didn't notice when Old Loco trotted off to bother a big-eyed cow.

He stopped rock still when he heard the dry, rattling sound just beyond his feet. The cacti spines dug in, tugging mercilessly at his clothing and exposed flesh. Sweat dripped and trickled down and over his skin to settle stingingly in deep scratches and tears. The rattling sound vibrated in the air again, closer. Tommy Lee slowly let his eyes travel downward. Not one, not two, but three large rattlers had been peacefully sleeping in the cacti only to be rudely awakened by Tommy Lee. He looked at the snakes, looked at the cacti and dove out of the cacti expecting to meet Old Loco and even his maker. The one thing he never expected to see were the hooves of a paint pony inches from his nose. He slowly rose to his knees, now finding himself eye to eye with the pony itself. Tommy Lee ducked his head to the side to see the rider of the pony and nearly swallowed the last of his chaw.

He carefully stood up. The rider shifted in his saddle then with a smug little smile said, "I still don't like you for kicking me, but my Ma says I should act like a man and forget it. Well, for now I just might forget it, seeing you need a ride…" the boy grinned at his little joke "My pony is real strong, he can carry us both." Tommy Lee stood there glaring at the boy. It was a good eight miles back to the ranch, his boots blistering him before that. Besides that, every bone in his body ached and he could tell he'd left the cacti patch with more than a few souvenirs.

If he'd thought coming into the ranch, yard belly down across a whelp's-size paint would rub against his pride, he'd been wrong. He'd tried to ride the whelp's pony back like a man ought too, only to find just where the cacti had left its mementos. Now here he was, face down on what had been Old Man Simms big oak fancy eating table. Face down with his pants and drawers down around his ankles and his lily-white backside in view for all of God and country to see. The boss lady was in the kitchen, boiling water and giving orders like some general to her whelps to tear clean rags into bandages. She had shut the big sliding doors to the room, set the younger whelps to work and ordered the eighteen year old girl child out of the room. Tommy Lee had been glad she'd done that—ordered the girl child out. The last time he'd seen anything with that hungry of a look in its eyes was when he'd come across a starved mountain cat.

He could tell by the giggles and choked laughter, that several of the whelps were taking turns at the keyhole. Suddenly he heard them scatter and the big doors slid open. The boss lady and one of the older male whelps were standing there.

"Well, Mr. Tommy Lee there's only one way that I know of to rid you of those cacti spines." The boss lady stood there wearing man's pants and a man's shirt, all of which were molded to her slim figure just a bit too tight, he thought. She held up a pair of needle nose pliers. "If you know of another way to get those things out you better tell me now."

He swallowed hard gritting his teeth, "No ma'am, I don't, and I'd be obliged if you get it over with as quick as you can."

She told one boy Billy Bob to hold Tommy Lees legs. "I am sorry it has to be me doing this, but as you know," Tommy Lee and the boss lady each grunted as she yanked the first spine out. "the rest of the hands are out rounding up the cattle." Some 23 spines later, his backside looking like he'd caught a round of buckshot, the boss lady gave him a draw of good sipping whiskey before she swabbed him down with the rest. She gave the pan with the spines and water to Billy Bob, telling him to take them out to the trash heap. Turning to Tommy Lee, she said, "I don't think you'll be doing much work for a few days. Matter of fact, I don't think you'll be wearing britches for the next few days either. Those wounds will need tending to twice a day, and with every hand working the round up, I guess the only place for you to stay is here at the house." He buried his head in his hands and groaned.

Every day for the past five, the boss lady had come in twice a day to make sure his backside hadn't started to fester. He shook his head over that; it wasn't his backside that was festering. Maybe it was being cooped up in this room, or maybe it was because the days had warmed up and the nights were even warmer, or maybe it was that piece-of-meat-on-a-hook feeling he got whenever that oldest girl child, Sally May, came in to check on him. Or maybe it was because the boss lady's clothes looked tighter every time, he saw her. Whatever the reason, he just couldn't take lying face down for another night. He rolled over and grimaced as he wiggled to find a comfortable position.

Tommy Lee was just starting to dream, he was at Miss Virginia's sporting house and that sweet Carol Ann, all soft and all full of curves, was shimming out of her shift. He ran his hands down her back, enjoying the feel of her rump filling his hands. He sighed as she straddled his hips, settling herself snugly there. He groaned happily as the female form changed into that of the boss lady's. His next few moments of bliss were shattered, and his eyes flew open when he heard, "Ride me Tommy Lee, ride me like you've somewhere to go!" And the voice was not that of the boss lady's, or Carol Ann's.

Tommy Lee stood there in his Sunday clothes, trying not to tug at his collar. It felt as tight as a noose, and he thought a hanging might be better than this. Old man Simms had once said a man of Tommy Lee's age should be putting down roots. He had scoffed at the old man's words, and at other hands who put down roots. Yup, he enjoyed his freedom. Whenever he'd felt like it, he'd pulled up stakes and taken off for greener pastures. He'd never liked real responsibility. Just do his job and when the urge struck, pack up his bed roll and move on. Oh, Duke, where are you? The music began and everyone stood up. He broke out in sweat, and it wasn't from the cold metal pressed into his side; he remembered that night. The door to his room had shook as it was kicked open, a lamp held high, blinded him momentarily before it was set down on a table with a thud. And then he heard the words that sealed his fate.

"Billy Bob get my shot gun! Jimmy Roy ride your paint over to the preacher's house and tell him there's going to be a wedding. And you…Mr.

Tommy Lee…for the time being…get your hands off my daughter!"

Message in a Bottle

THE SUN TIPPED toed through the tree tops sliding down their trunks to the forest floor spreading its light. Midnight mist swirled and danced away to allow another day's morn.

Sarafina, a multicolored shawl wrapped around her shoulders leaned against the open door's jam to her cottage. A mug of her favorite morning tea, steam rising, warmed her hands.

Crows cried greetings to the woodland creatures and her. She lifted her drink in a return salute. A tug at her vibrant skirts hem made her smile. Sarafina bent down and scooped up the tiny long-haired, deer-head, Chihuahua with her free hand.

"Good morning, Max." The little dog whimpered and nuzzled her chin. Next, he growled the cutest puppy sound. She cuddled him closer.

"I'll keep you safe from her but someday you'll have to stand up for yourself."

He relaxed in the crook of her arm and sighed. A sign that wouldn't be today.

A bump against her leg alerted her to the terror which had had Max running for safety.

"Really, Toby, don't be such a POS to him. He's still a baby, be nice." The one-eyed, notched ear, one and a half-fanged cat wound around her legs before setting herself at Sarafina's feet. A saucy meow, almost a feline chuckle drifted upward. The pup tried to be good, but he was still a baby. He loved to chase the cat, and the cat loved to egg him on with her fluffy twitching tail. Sarafina was sure, well pretty sure Toby really wouldn't hurt him. But Max did look like a big mouse and Toby was an excellent hunter. The lack of snakes, mice and other creepy crawlies attained to her prowess. There once were other cats in the area, but Toby chased them off, establishing her own queendom.

A warning cry from the crows perched around the cottage filled the air. Some hopped from branch to branch agitated. Their leader Tomkin was down by the pond. His attention was on something in the water.

Tomkin pecked at it cawing a warning to the

object. Sarafina put her mug down, tied her shawl into a sling and deposited Max safely in the folds. Toby was purring a bit too loud this morning, a sure sign of mischief to come and an indication not to put the puppy anywhere near her.

Grabbing a handful of food for the crows, corn, other seeds, berries and nuts she spread them on the ground. A ritual she'd done for years. She helped feed and shelter them and they warned her of trespassers and left her trinkets.

Tomkin still at the water's edge, fretted before spreading his black wings to flap twice and lifted gracefully upward. He then landed at her feet dropping a glittering green bottle.

"Why thank you, Tomkin. I hope you like your breakfast. I added the pumpkin seeds you love."

The bird cawed a thanks and hopped away. Sarafina bent to pick up the gift uncorking the vessel. Inside a note nestled there, her nimble fingers worked the message free. Strange, it was addressed to her, and she began to read. 'Dear Sarafina, we've been trying to reach you about your extended warranty.'

Hidden Truth

THE HOWLING AND screams bombarded her ears. The Goddess clapped her hands over them and hunched over from the pain of the assault. Why, were her children wailing and attacking each other?

Donning her cloak of humanity, she raced down to earth. She first went to the cities. There she found people huddled in their boxes fearful to go out. The streets overflowed with violence and hate. Next, she went to the suburbs again, the people huddled in their bigger boxes barely venturing out and only to the small spaces of green they claimed as theirs.

The Goddess roamed to the forests of the few that were left. She sat down and began to weep. The sky darkened and her tears poured from the clouds. Day turned into night and back to the next morn and still she cried.

And then she heard it, laughter.

Children laughing.

Two, one boy, one girl, one light, one dark.

Laughing, giggling, running down the muddy path, jumping in the puddles.

All the while joyous.

They held hands and walked up to her.

Unafraid, offering a few wildflowers of yellow, purple and white.

"For me?" she whispered.

"For you. Granny says flowers always make a lady smile and you look like you need both."

"Thank you."

"Are you hungry? Granny is making stew can't you smell it?"

The Goddess lifted her chin giving a delicate sniff with her nose. "Why yes, I can. Do you think she'll have enough for another person? A stranger?"

The children took her hand pulling her up, "Of course, we always have enough. You're not a stranger we just hadn't met you yet."

They led her down a path filled now with sunshine and muddy puddles which they tried every one. To a ramshackle building they called home. An old woman in a many mended dress a ancient shawl possibly as old as her warmed her thin shoulders.

"Welcome, welcome my dear. Come share some food, drink, conversation and laughter with us."

Men and women came from the woods and pulled their boats from the water all bringing something to add to the cast iron pot nestled on a fire.

Young, old, somewhere in between, some with canes, many with strong backs, some with babies on their hips. The babies were passed around given many hugs and kisses all adored.

As the night crept in and stomachs were filled, blankets were brought out to ward off the chill. A fire to warm and draw out the music and stories glowed.

The Goddess was accepted into their fold as family which she was.

In the morning, she slipped away filled with renewed hope and love for her children. There were still more who shared what little they had without wanting in response. There was still good in her world.

The Secret

IN THE MIDDLE of the park is a small, weathered stone. Long ago, the words inscribed on it had blurred. Now, people make up stories of what was once written there. Some say it was nothing more than a milestone proclaiming the distance from one town to the next. Others thought it to be the grave marker of the founding father of the town. And some say it marked the location of a great and ancient battle.

None are correct, but then how could they be? For I alone know its true meaning, since 'twas I that carved the words and placed the stone where it now rests, many lifetimes' past.

The river below the bluff where the stone resides once spanned a width that would take a man an entire sweep of a clock's hand to cross. Now, it could be crossed by a man in one quarter of that time. When I carved the stone and placed it on the bluff, man told time not by clocks, only by the movement of the sun.

Man.

I have seen him grow and can only hope time and maturity will make him wiser than he is now. When first I met him, he was a squalling child who disliked sharing, causing petty fighting all around him. The man I see now is a blustering, swaggering, self-involved yearling. I do not like this man. Should he survive this period of his growth perhaps he will turn into a seasoned, more polished man. If he does, I think I would take the time to sit and talk with him more.

Over the passing of time, I have known one or two men who were advanced in their thinking. These men I befriended, sharing some of my knowledge.

But I must confess, it has been the women I have most admired and enjoyed. They are the ones with the greatest patience and wisdom. While their men go off to hunting, to warring, to their many 'man' things, the women stay rooted to bear and raise the seeds planted in them. Women watch the ways of men, then start the evolving, correcting process in the offspring. It may take them much time before progress will be seen, but there—will—be—progress.

I digress. I was telling of the stone. It honors a great, fiery, independent spirit. One whose abundant, gleaming ebony waves of curls caught the light from a campfire and my eye late one night. It was a time for me when changing my appearance was as easy as changing my cap. The spirit who resided in a body of gentle rounded curves, soft delicious swells and enticing hollows taught me much. It allowed me to feel its loneliness and share mine with it, easing the pain within each of us.

I stayed a fortnight with this spirit, loving it as only man can love. When the time came for me to leave, the spirit did not weep or wail. It did not lament or condemn. It only kissed my cheek and bade me a safe journey.

I did not know then, but the spirit held a secret, one that I would not know of 'til a long time passed. Being new to the physical flesh-trappings of man, I knew not of what I entrusted to the spirit. Had I known of the spirit's secret I would have stayed, but then, perhaps the spirit knew this and kept silent purposely. As it was, the spirit enlisted the aid of a great king to twice deliver the secret. First into one world, then into another. There the secret grew and flourished into a master of its own realm, never knowing about its gypsy or *demon* heritage.

The spirit went deep into the night until last I found it. Cold and tired it was. I held it, warmed it, and tucked it into its bed for an eternal sleep. I did not weep or wail or lament or condemn, for it would not have asked that I did.

It was for myself, and perhaps the secret, I carved and left the stone on that high bluff. The stone covers what once was the *physical*, the spirit has long since departed.

But with or without that ancient stone, I will remember a spirit with a scarlet full mouth, dark dancing eyes and the secret we share.

Winifred Elizabeth Waters

Winifred Elizabeth Waters was a quiet woman who grew up as an only child in a loving but well-structured household of elderly parents. The body's nourishment was consumed at six, twelve, and six every day. Sundays were the exception to this rule when a small slice of pie or cake with one scoop, no more, of ice cream, could be eaten at seven in the evening. Every item had a place in the home and shouldn't be anywhere else. Ladies, she was reminded daily, wore their skirts to mid-calf and cuffs and collars were always buttoned. A straight spine and squared shoulders made a lady's appearance with perfectly coiffed hair and makeup to accent not announce a woman's features. All demeanor of an educated, wellborn woman.

When her parents passed, she was lost at sea in

the search for someone, hopefully a husband, to love and spend her life. Then she met Stewart Albert Pendragon Buckley.

He was a new employee at Henson, Henson, Calamount, and Lloyd, the law firm where Winifred was a secretary to the first Mr. Henson. Stewart was an up-and-coming attorney on the fast track to associate partner.

One morning at a breakfast meeting Stewart made sure that a pair of roses were next to her plate of eggs Benedict. How romantic, Winifred thought. Eggs and roses.

In the next few weeks shy glances during meetings, a brush of fingertips when handing papers to each other made Winifred's pulse quicken. Oh, Winifred was falling hard for this man. Then Stewart was promoted and received a corner office for his hard work, an office with its own bathroom no less. Winifred collected her own promotion to girlfriend of Mr. Stewart Albert Pendragon Buckley announced by a two-dozen bouquet of red roses on her desk.

Oh, how excited she was, this man was the impeccable gentleman she thought in all ways. He bore the key to the treasure of her heart. Then one day shortly thereafter, Winifred while delivering papers to her beau's office and placing the files on his desk, turned to leave and the open door to the bathroom drew her attention. Her hand flew to her buttoned throat; a tiny gasp slipped from her perfectly glossed lips. No, no, her mind screamed as a tiny tear hung at the corner of one eye before tumbling down her cheek.

The man she believed to be complete in all ways in his Brooks Brothers suites and well-set hair combed just so to one side and flawless manners was a fraud! Stewart Albert Pendragon Buckley was appallingly guilty in Ms. Winifred Elizabeth Waters' tidy mind of the ultimate horror…he left the toilet seat up.

POETRY

CHICKENS

This is dedicated to our great-grandson, Daxton, who inspired me.

Chickens, Chickens
Dancing to festive little tunes
Wearing fancy pantaloons
Eating pretty macaroons
Chickens, chickens
Singing little songs
Traipsing off to town
To buy the most potato skins
Dripping in saucy cheese
Chickens, chickens
Happy little birds.

WHO AM I?

Who am I?
I squint at the world,
worry mars my brow.
What century is this?
Or better yet, what day or hour?
A fierce daughter who sits by a quiet lake,
listening to crow cry,
prophecies ancient and babe new.
I see the world,
Oceans of deep cobalt,
meadows of sunshine Dahlias.
The scent of new borns tickles my nose,
as does decaying society resides.
Mirth burst from between broken lips.
Tears of shattered glass
bleed and scars,

my body and heart.
I cast white stones,
and chicken bones
as the rat doctor looks on.
His top hat askew,
beady eyes and sharp teeth belie a false intent,
tainted words no comfort spews forth.
My eyes dim from the fog of time.
Memories, treasured children's smiles,
coo to me.
Eternal cessation promised.
Coffins' sleep
descends.
Who am I?
Does it matter?

Valentines Not One Day a Year

Coffee made by her hand,
Tea made by his hand,
Aroma of coffee brewing fills the air,
Tea darkens as it steeps.
Crows calling in the skies and yard,
A gentle sound to wake the senses.
No scarlet flowers.
No sweetened candies.
No sparkling gems.
He sips his coffee,
She her tea.
Love is a shared secret smile,
Memories of a lifetime with more to come.
A quiet time spent together each day,
Knowing the other's silent repose.
Everyday is Valentines.

About the Author

Thank you for purchasing this labor of love, laughter, sweat, and tears. I hope this book brings you happiness and joy, and maybe a hearty giggle. If you would like to read more of my work, go to: www.amazon.com.

J. Paulette Forshey is an award-winning, internationally recognized author based in Ohio, where she lives with her husband and a Chihuahua. She specializes in writing romance novels across various sub-genres, including paranormal, contemporary, thriller, fantasy, and erotica. Her works often reflect her creative versatility and passion for storytelling. Some of her notable titles include *The Tarczal Alliance*, *Miracles From The Heart*, and contributions to anthologies like *Three to Tango II*. Forshey's writing journey began after her sons graduated high school, encouraged by her husband, who also serves as the inspiration for her romantic heroes. For more details about her and her books, you can visit her official website at www.jpauletteforshey.com.

www.ingramcontent.com/pod-product-compliance
Lightning Source LLC
LaVergne TN
LVHW010700110826
845149LV00014B/3177

* 9 7 9 8 9 9 4 5 9 9 7 0 9 *